Tales from the Perseus Arm Volume 1

Edited by

Sam Taylor

ISBN (Electronic): 978-0-9925415-6-9
ISBN (Print):   978-0-9925415-7-6

Tales from the Perseus Arm

Volume 1

(a science fiction anthology)

Take a small group of hand-picked new science fiction authors chosen from over 3,000 writers from the US, UK, Germany, Ireland, and Australia. Ask them each to write a science fiction short story. Invite famous UK author John Gribbin to contribute. Discover an exciting up-and-coming cover artist, Patricia Burn.

Put it all together and you have the stunning new science fiction anthology, *Tales from the Perseus Arm*. It is a collection of 10 original stories about robots, aliens, the depths of space, the astounding future and the sometimes troubling things that happen to the humans who have to cope with all of this. *Tales from the Perseus Arm* is fresh and original and will enchant both existing and new science fiction fans alike. We had enormous fun writing this, and we hope that you will have just as much fun reading it.

Edited by Sam Taylor

Contents

SPACE CADET
By Patricia Burn

Trembling like a leaf
engulfed in the
volcanic eruption of
plasma-fire
and the hideous
unmanning
noise of Death
stands the boy.

"We'll make a man of him, Ma'am"
they'd said.

But now
the boy's a jackrabbit
mesmerised
he stands exposed
along the dotted line
his mother signed upon,
hypnotised
by the one blind eye
that has him firmly in its sights
as he waits
rigid
for it to
wink.

Edited by Sam Taylor

SHIPPING AND HANDLING
By Salvatore B Lombard

The pod opened with a hiss.

A pale gas trickled up out of it, drifting up to dissipate against the harsh operating lights. The sensors began to beep. The wallscreen flickered on and data started to stream, listing temperatures and life readings, filling up the panel with flickering lights and codes.

The Robal peered into the pod. It gripped the broken edges and wedged them wider open, allowing light to penetrate down and illuminate a tiny golden creature. It was curled tight into itself, tiny spurs clasping it shut. It held a sheen like metal and gave off an odor that the computer registered as mixed rosemary and ancient motor oil.

The Robal took two clamps from under the table and used them to hold the pod open. It reached down with two gripping limbs to grasp the small creature, twisting its own face away from the open capsule as if to avoid the smell, and retrieved the little gold thing from it.

It laid down a plush towel on the table and placed the creature upon it. The Robal had to peel its appendages from the thing's skin, making a tiny disgusted noise at the fibrous strings that clung to it. It wiped its digits on its apron and reached up for the detachable showerhead. Pressing a few buttons, it set the acid levels and gave a few experimental squeezes of the hand lever, shooting little spurts of green liquid in the sink. The liquid hissed when it hit the metal and left a rusty tinge behind as it ran into the drain.

Satisfied, the Robal bent once more over the gold thing. It adjusted the flow to a mere misting and pumped the hand lever, hovering the showerhead over the creature. There was a quiet puff puff as the liquid was dispersed. Green droplets grew on the golden skin.

At first, nothing happened. Then there was a soft clicking, and the coiled creature began to unfurl like a fern. The hard skin rippled with a series of clacks, as layers of thin armor shifted underneath, the metal plates readjusting to allow it to uncoil. The green drops seemed to seep through, leaving pinkish dull spots on the otherwise glistening hide.

As it came out of its coil, the creature revealed its shape. It had four limbs, tiny nubby legs that seemed unable to support its body. It had a short tail nearly identical to those limbs. And its head was a large wedge, which curled out from under its chest, its two large inkblot eyes blinking under the bright lights. It was almost fetal in appearance. Definitely infantile, with baby like pudge on its stomach and cheeks. Its head nosed about, seemed to sniff the towel, and lifted up to peep at the Robal.

A drop of the green liquid fell upon its blunt nose and the little creature squealed. It made a dash off the towel - it was surprisingly fast for its proportions. The Robal seized the creature and slammed it down with a crack of its digits. Holding the wriggling creature down with two limbs, it raised the showerhead with a third and adjusted the settings with a fourth. It increased the spray and held it down over the creature's face. The little thing writhed, poking out from between two grips, tossing wildly about. It squealed and squealed as the green flowed over it, hissing as it went.

Finally the creature ceased to move. The Robal turned off the flow, shaking the last drops from the showerhead and putting it back up on its hook. The Robal turned the gold thing on its back and prodded its soft underbelly experimentally. When there was no reaction, it peeled back a sheath on one of its digits, revealing a pointed spur. It dug that spur into the golden flesh and pulled with a riiiiip.

Having created a hole, it sheathed the spur and dug its digits into the gap, pulling until the skin tore. The Robal peeled it away in great strips and flaps, discarding the golden pieces on the floor where they curled up like sheets of wallpaper.

Soon the little creature was no longer golden. It was naked and pink, protected only by a series of large scales along its back, which the Robal proceeded to tear off and discard as well. They clattered to the ground alongside the skin.

When it lay bare, limp and pink and glistening as all things freshly shelled or skinned, the Robal picked it up. It held the creature dangling loosely, pinched between the tips of two digits, holding it away from its own body. It popped open the top of a nearby incubator and tossed the thing down into it. It slammed shut the lid, punched a button, and bent to look through the transparent siding.

The creature stirred. It lifted its fat head, wriggled its tiny nubby digits, and looked about. Clear liquid beaded up at the points where its armor had been torn away and trickled in small drops down its side.

It wobbled up to the side and poinked the clear wall with its nose. The Robal flicked a lever. The incubator made a whummmm sound and began to shake. The little creature in it staggered around like it was in an earthquake. Another little lever, and a light came on, and a little port on the top began to show the rising temperature, from 70 jumping to 75 and then 80 and up and up in 5 degree increments until it had climbed up to 110. The little creature seemed to sweat, more clear liquid rolling over it, and when the port hit 115 there was a loud WHUMP as its eyeballs swelled, blew out of its head, and hit the wall. Its whole body began to swell up like a pink marshmallow.

The Robal pushed a button, and the sides of the box changed to a pleasant (and opaque) medium blue. The Robal straightened up, adjusted the humidity, and then touched a button on its own torso.

"677," said a sharp voice, from a speaker in the Robal's side. "732! 856! 125!"

The Robal jiggled a kind of tuner that sat alongside the speaker.

"-ready yet? Waiting for days now-"

"Package was late to deliver," said the Robal. "Casings now just removed, settings fix, now warming."

"You mean you just started?" the voice almost screamed.

"Soon made," said the Robal. "Process of man three hours."

It pushed another button and the voice stopped.

"Nagging housefly," said the Robal, under its breath. It turned back to the incubator and pushed a button, and the screen became see-through once more.

The once-little creature was now enormously swollen, so that it was crammed within the box with little room, its face squashed up against the front above two feet, which now resembled hands, with a number of finger like digits splayed against the screen.

Its mouth opened and closed against the wall, but there was no sound. A row of blunt teeth were visible growing in behind its lips. Its eye sockets gaped, eyelids crumpling inward with no ball to curl around. It had a nose growing; little more than a slightly raised lump with two slits in it. Little shell ears had begun to bud on the sides of its increasingly round head.

The Robal tapped experimentally on the glass. The creature started, rubbed its face around on the siding, and seemed to mouth at the Robal's fingerdigits.

Satisfied, the Robal set a timer and went to its plush chair. It pulled out a much-tattered magazine from where it was wedged under the cushion, put up two of its feet, and with a covert look around began to read.

When the timer finally went off, with a loud BLARRRRR the Robal was visibly startled, dropping its magazine with a guilty air and slapping off the timer.

It flipped up the incubator lid and reached in. It felt hair and wrapped its digits in it to grab and pull the creature out. The thing emerged squealing, its new face screwed up in pain.

The hair had grown atop its head, stopping at the neck and skirting the face and ears. Its nose had grown fully, nostrils and cartilage and all, and lips had formed around its gaping red hole of a mouth, which opened wide now in a squall that displayed tongue and blunt teeth.

The Robal released it, and the creature fell to the tile, scrabbling clumsily with hands and fingers that twitched from lack of use.

Counting, the Robal found five fingers on each hand; the proper number.

Its body was much thinned and elongated, bone and tissue outlined in new beige skin. Its hind legs had grown way out, spindly and with knees now, bowlegged and trying (and failing) to regain control. The Robal counted the toes on the flat feet; five.

Shifting its vision readout, the Robal found one brain, large and forever folding in on itself, one heart, pumping like mad. Two lungs. Spleen, liver, kidneys, stomach, large and small intestine. And the bones were all there, the proper number of ribs, the hipbones, the humerus, the pelvis, the skull. It counted ligaments and muscles and fat and eventually concluded that everything was in good order. Except…

The Robal pulled out a door and scrabbled around in it, discarding pens and clipboards and spanners. It made a clicking noise when it finally found and grabbed what it was looking for. It unscrewed the lid off a small round container, peeled off the seal, and fished around in thick, smelly liquid until it found two squelchy orbs.

Pinning the pink creature down, and ignoring its screams, the Robal pushed up the loose eyelids and wedged a fresh eye into each socket.

When released, the creature rolled on the floor, covering its face with its hand and making mad screaming noises. It wept clear and greenish fluid, which ran down its cheeks and dripped onto the tile. Its whole body was consumed with tremors.

"Record: normal, healthy response," said the Robal.

"Whu- whu- whu-" said the beige creature. It lifted its head at the Robal, squinting and blinking away the green tears. "What- what- what a-are yo-" It couldn't seem to finish its attempt at speech and abruptly gagged, turning away and retching clear bile on the floor. It coughed and wiped its mouth and made a horrible moaning noise.

"Inquiry," said the Robal. "Able to see?" It pulled the creature's hands away from its face. "Color vision? Both sufficient?"

"Let go of me!" snarled the creature. It wormed away from the Robal, twisting clumsily on the floor as if its limbs were jelly.

"Answer insufficient," said the Robal. It pulled the creature back by its ankle, ignoring its kicking. "Able to see? Please give reply."

"I can see your ugly face!" the creature screamed. "Now let me go!"

"Answer, satisfactory." The Robal released the creature's leg and let it squirm away, huddling away under a counter. The Robal pressed the button on its torso again and the speakway screeched to life. "Announce," it said. "Man grown, condition satisfactory, rate nine out of ten, 'would definitely buy again'."

"It's alive?"

"Yes."

"Are you sure? Did you check to see if it's breathing? You know you forgot about the breathing last time-"

"Checked respiration," said the Robal. "Checked circulation. Checked brain action and acquired vocal response for purpose of certainty."

"Oh, it's talking then? Bring it over and let me hear it."

The Robal took the creature by its foot again, dragging it out from under the counter. It clawed on the floor and made many screechy noises. The Robal pulled its head by the hair up to its metallic chest. "Speak," it said. "Require vocal check."

The creature said nothing and struggled to get free.

"Robal," said the voice from the speaker. "Robal! Make it talk!"

The Robal twisted its ear and the creature shrieked. "Let go of me!" it yelled. "Let go!"

"Ooh, it sounds lively," said the speaker. "Now, Robal, I want you to take care with it- if you squash another I will fire you! Remember, they're almost extinct, and I don't want to shell out another fifty grand to have one shipped deep-space. You understand me?"

"Perfect understanding, madam," said the Robal.

"Good," said the voice, and there was a click, and the speaker turned off. The Robal tuned itself down and released the creature, which immediately crawled away again, back to its under-the-counter hole. The Robal leaned over to peep at it.

"Inquiry," it said. "Require sustenance? Require void bladder?"

"What?" asked the creature, peering suspiciously back at it.

"Sustenance, vitals, food, edibles," the Robal began to rattle off.

"If I eat anything I'll puke again," it said, rubbing its fresh eyes and making sniffly noises.

"Required to ingest water," said the Robal. "Deep-space process drain of bodily fluids, necessitate hydration." It reached across a countertop and took a bag of fluid from a rack, drawing a needle and a long tube from another drawer. It dangled these implements in front of the pink creature's face. "If not ingest independently, apply force-hydration."

"Okay," said the creature quickly. "Do you have bottled water? I can't drink tap."

The Robal discarded the hydration implements, opened a nearby fridge door, and got the creature its water. It cracked off the lid and placed it before the creature's little refuge, where it reached out and took it in still-quivering fingers. Water spilled everywhere but the creature managed to ingest most of what had been in the bottle. When that was done, finding itself still thirsty, the creature licked spare drops from its hands and arms. The Robal got it another bottle.

Drinking, the creature watched warily as the Robal busied itself about the room, fiddling with various instruments.

"Who are you?" it asked. "Where am I?"

"Assigned name 6034674305uasl23063, but no require formal, basic title Robal. Present location starship Radon Edifier, under captainship of most respected Lady of Star of Dust, ambassador of Oon, currently hostess to Starturan Msk of Third Star Motan." The Robal picked up a pair of metallic pincers, looked from them to the pink creature, then put them down. It then picked up and considered a sharper implement shaped like a question mark. "Inquiry: count yourself as among human race? Born period of 7.12 on planet of Terra Forma?"

"Yeah, until the raiders invaded our settlement." The creature looked nervously at the implement. "Are we close to there? I don't remember anything – was I rescued? What star system are we in?"

"Negative. Negative. Binarium, halfway between moonlets of Kardy and Malcum."

"How did I get here?"

The Robal paused, antennae whirring, and then retracted a few steps to the counter still holding the remains of the pod. It lifted up a mass of carefully folded paper, opening it like origami from a small bud to a wide star of folds, skimming one metallic digit down the paper until it landed on the relevant square. " 'Subject was found afloat in small pod, midspace between Cardiff and region of meteoric rain,' " it read aloud. " 'All signs indicate that raider jet was obliterated by enemy rays and stock expelled into space, subject among it. Subject was carefully preserved via genetic compression and held in stock for you, favored customer, until you should have need of it. Specimen appeared to be male, in good health, and lacking dangerous levels of environmental toxins.' "

"Genetic compression?" the creature repeated. "What the

hell is genetic compression?"

"Method of preservation lasting centuries, pioneered by the Zytophans."

"The Zytophans!" The creature sat up so quick that it almost struck its head on the bottom of its cubby. "But the Zytophans are scrub! A slave race! No better than plankton, with no concept of any kind of science!"

"Zytophans are noble race of humble origin," said the Robal. "Evolved through many generation to pinnacle of achievement."

"Evolved? That's impossible..." The creature trailed off, and then a horrible thought occurred to it. "Robal? What year is it?"

"Adjusting for your time scale? Unknown. Many many century past time of your species. Very few specimen remain. My mistress, very clever, very fortunate, to locate such specimen."

"Very few," said the creature through numb lips. "Many century." It huddled back into its cubby and wrapped its arms around itself, face going ghostlike. "You mean, you mean-" It did not finish its sentence but began to rock back and forth with an uncomprehending expression. Its mouth went into an o shape and stayed silent.

The Robal turned on its speaker. "Madam," it said. "Specimen displaying signs of stress, vitals becoming irregular. Recommend action?"

"Do not involve me in such trivial matters, Robal!" snapped the voice. "Follow the instructions I gave you, and interrupt me no more! I am entertaining the ambassador. Do you understand?!"

"Perfect understanding, madam," said the Robal.

"Good," said the voice, and then it blipped off.

The Robal tuned down its speakway and picked up the sharp, question-mark-shaped instrument. It reached under the counter and pulled out the pink creature, which shivered and batted at the Robal's fingerdigits with no success. The Robal brought the instrument up above its head and thwacked it down. There was a horrible squeal. The Robal lifted it up, its tip shining freshly red in the fluorescent lights, and then brought it down again.

Thwack. Squeal.

Thwack. Squeal.

Thwack. Silence.

The Robal dropped the bloodied implement in the sink and dragged the creature's limp body across the room. It left a snailtrail of blood behind on the white tile. The Robal wiped red dribble from the creature's lips, snot from its nose, and hauled the body up onto a slotted silver tray. The Robal opened a drawer. It fished about, clicking to itself, until it found a number of long pins. It used these to thrust through the creature's joints, holding it secure, and tied its hands and feet to the wide tray with a flexible tan wire. It pried opened its mouth and, fishing in a refrigerated drawer, took a soft pulsing egg and thrust it between the creature's lips. It took green filaments and shredded them over the creature's back. It snipped off and discarded the ears.

The Robal stepped back to examine its handiwork. It scrutinized the body, nodded, and slid the tray off the counter. Staggering under its weight, it wobbled over to a wheelie cart and placed the tray atop. It brushed its bloody fingerdigits on its apron and then pushed the cart across the room. A set of doors whooshed apart and then slid back together after the Robal had passed.

The halls were alive with Gans, running along underfoot toting gas rings, cackling and shouting at each other, blasting little scorch marks on the walls. They barked as the Robal approached and scattered to allow its passing.

"603! 603!" said a voice. A familiar headorb poked out of a nearby wallslot. "678 875 001?"

"345 324," said the Robal.

"Check," it said, and disappeared back into the wiring.

The Robal wheeled onwards. One of the wheels of the cart needed oiling and squeaked loudly as it went. The tail of it kept catching on the carpet.

Three turns took the Robal and its burden to a set of wide doors, reaching high above its head, layered with scales and old gems. The key creature glared at the Robal and rattled its ring. "You're late," it said. "Passcode?"

"3.14159625," said the Robal.

"Ha ha," the key creature sneered. "Very funny." It swung the doors open anyway, and the Robal wheeled onwards.

The chamber was plush with fur, from the walls to the ceiling, and to the Robal's scent receptors smelled like a mixture of mating fluid and printing oil. At the end of the chamber was a great couch, laden with eggs, and among them lay the Ambassador herself, resplendent in her natural oils and a glowing status pin on her left chest. "Well, finally," she said when she noticed him. "We were beginning to think that you had set the kitchen afire."

Starturan Msk, sitting to her right and dwarfed by the surrounding eggs, looked up. "Oh, splendid!" he said, wriggling his nose. "You know, madam, I half believed you were joking about the human."

"I never joke," she said, and clapped her hands. "Thank you as ever for your service, Robal. Sir, let us take a brief respite from our business. Dinner, is served!"

Edited by Sam Taylor

BLUMELENA
By Rachael Kelly

- LMAO @ pris
- StokeyBoy, why dont u keep ur opinions 2 urself? No1 want 2 hear.
- OOOOOO sorrrrry!!!!!! U got ur period or what?
- now now girls.
- LMFAO @ rob1277

A stream of letters, trickling rainbow-hued down a page too small to hold them. Leo enters the room with his usual vigour.

- HHHHEEEEEELLLLOOOO RRRROOOOOOMMMMMMMMMM!!!!!!!!!!!!!!!!!!!!!

He knows some of them. They greet him like a friend.

- not so loud, LionKing – pris have hangover
- *gives pris beer*
- up urs Stokey.
- LOL @ Stokey. I'll have beer if pris dosnt want 1
- lion u been floating in room 4 10 mins or so. What u doin – hiding?

He smiles. When he pictures DiamondDel he sees a forty-year-old man with greasy hair in need of an inch or so lopping off, alone in a darkened room while his Mum watches The X-Factor downstairs. Diamond is paranoia's paranoiac; his text oozes distrust.

- keepin eye on u, diamond. What's up?
- Long time no c, lionking. U avoiding us?
- U wish, stokey.
- Pity 4 pris, pris not well
- *hugs pris* Better?
- <smileyface> lion ur a gent

He hasn't been online for ten days, not since he promised himself a life and actual human interaction. He's been to cinemas and museums and discovered that the screen remains regardless. People are a step removed from each other, separated by a line of fibre optic cable or an inability to catch another's eye: it's all the same. Human interaction is a myth. Leo is happier where he is.

During the day, he draws pictures of them, of who he imagines them to be. Pris is a whiner: he sees her as a narrow, dark-haired girl, mid- to late-twenties, but the face of a teenager. She smokes and she wears too much make-up. She's lonely, but, like Leo, like all of them, her doors are all locked and she doesn't have a key. She was hungover last time he was online, she's hungover again today. He wonders if she has a problem, or if she pretends for attention.

Stokey has a vicious streak. He's a fat kid, a virgin, who reads fantasy novels because they're more real to him than life. He floats through his day, convinced he's still dreaming. He has a genius IQ and a crop of acne as red and violent as the surface of Venus. He'd like to disappear, but he's too bloody-minded. Moon_fish isn't among them tonight, but give her an hour or so. Moon_fish keeps irregular hours: Leo thinks she has a baby or a young family, but she denies it.

He chats for a while. They talk about films he suspects they haven't seen, websites he opens in a kaleidoscope of tabs while he types. He'd like to ask them, what do you think about at night, when you can't sleep and the world is silent and black? But he doesn't. He says, ne1 seen Moon?

dosen't luv us ne more, says pris.

He thinks it's a shot at him, but he lets it pass. The adminbot writes,

< Bloom has entered the room>

The name catches his eye. Bloom: it has an innocence that he likes, as though the bearer were a little too pure for their sophisticated ennui. He writes,

Hi, Bloom. How u doing?

Before she can reply, Stokey writes,

- don't talk to her, she mental.

He can sense the newcomer wilting, her colour fading. He writes,

22

stokey, u ever the gent. I put u on ignore now shut up.

Bloom says – OK – u?

- good, he says. – Where u frm?

- birmingham. U?

- london.

It's a lie. He lives in Belfast, but it's too longstanding to contradict. Last year, pris asked him for nightclub recommendations for a trip she was taking to his pretend suburb, and he had to spend three hours researching them on the internet.

- u like birmingham? he says. He's not sure why it's hard to talk to her, why he's constructed such a fragile, tender image in his head after nine words of conversation.

- OK, she says. – U like London?

He's never been. He says,

- love it. but is vv touristy these days. B.ham better, I think.

- U know B'ham?

- A little.

It's also a lie. He can't stop himself.

She says – have 2 go. C u later.

For a minute, he wonders if he's been caught out. Then he laughs at himself: he's turning into Diamond. He says,

- speak 2 u soon.

But before he can send it, the administrator writes,

< Bloom has left the room >

- told u she is mental, says Stokey.

*

Leo wanders, lonely, for an hour or so, listing aimlessly from site to site, feeling his eyes get heavy, his brain begin the gnawing buzz that will hold off sleep until just before he needs to wake up. He searches for sites on Birmingham, finds an online guide, looks at the What's On listing. Clubs, theatres, galleries fail to inspire him. He thinks about Bloom, wonders if she's a joiner-in or a fringe-hugger like him. Does she know these places? Does she visit them? Does she pretend to despise them so that no one will know that the reason she avoids them is because no one has asked her? He trails through flower sites in a variety of languages. If Bloom were a bloom, what bloom would she be? He flicks through white roses and lilies – too obvious – past sweeping hydrangea and psychedelic, tumbling fuschia. He decides at last on winter jasmine: frail and delicate, pretty at the wrong time.

*

Pris is getting advice on her love life from Moon_fish.

- I no hes not right 4 me, she says. Leo wonders if he exists.

- Do u thnk hes sorry? asks Moon, who sounds bored.

- Maybe. but hes always sorry.

- Chicks, eh? says Jazbo, who doesn't know them well enough to join in. Pris overreacts.

- Fuck u, Jazbo, she spits. – u no nthng about me, ok, so dont start

Leo considers leaving and signing in again under a different name, so he can tell pris to shut up.

- hi evry1, says Bloom.

She gets a chorus of hi's from people Leo doesn't know. Stokey says hi, but he follows it with an LOL. Leo says,

- Hi. Where did u go the other nite?

- Had to go, she says. – u want to PM?

Leo agrees. Stokey starts on him, but he puts him on ignore for a minute or two to cool him off. She opens with,

- U put stokeyboy on ignore?

- Yep, he says. – why?

- He's not happy.

- LMAO, he says. – It'll do him good.

- He's got a real problem with me, she says.

- Ignore him. How's life in B.ham?

- Same old. How's London?

- Can u keep a secret?

- Sure. Fire away.

- I don't live in London.

- Where do you live?

- Belfast.
- U like it?
- No.
- I won't tell anyone. My lips are sealed.

He takes StokeyBoy off ignore. The air turns blue. In the common room, he says,

- u kiss ur mother with that mouth, Stoke?

When he clicks back into the private room, Bloom is gone.

*

Every other Thursday, he signs on at the Benefits Office. The staff are pleasant but unrelenting. Leo protests: what's the point in applying when no-one ever calls back? The man on the counter offers him an unblinking stare and offers to take him through their list of admin positions.

- u work? he asks her.

There's a pause before she replies.

- what u mean?
- do u have a job, he explains, wondering, for the first time, if English isn't her native language.
- Sometimes, she says.

He can feel her getting evasive. He thinks, illegal immigrant? then changes his mind. Bloom confounds his every attempt to construct her; she's like fluid. Some days she's black-haired with hazelnut eyes; other days she's blond, Nordic. Sometimes she's tall and fine boned; other times she's birdlike. Today he has created her dark-skinned and exotic; tomorrow he will change his mind again. He says,

- what's ur real name?
- Bloom, she says.
- I'll tell u mine if u tell me urs.
- I like lion better, she says.
- It's leo, he tells her.
- What's leo?
- Me. Leo Devlin. I'm 30 yrs old. I like manga and red dwarf. I can quote whole sections of pratchett. My fav food is won ton soup. My fav colour is black. U?

Nothing. She is silent. He says again – what about u?

- blumelena, she says, and then she's gone.

*

Blumelena. He doesn't even know how to pronounce it, let alone what it might be, but in the space of minutes, of seconds, it has become her, the essence of her, her secret self. An ugly word – heavy and clumsy. A stocky Teutonic matron; a fortified house. Bloom, but not Bloom.

He calls up a search engine. Blumelena, he types. There are no results.

*

Is it a name? He pores over German sites, Hungarian sites, Russian sites: all curling tails and smooth bends, a language he can barely read but loves to look at. He calls up maps of Europe and beyond, hoping for a clue, some hint as to which of her many faces is the one she finally turns upon him. Hugging the Brazilian coast, north of São Paolo, he finds a town called Blumenau; in Nicaragua, a shanty town called Bluefields. Is it a book? Is it an anagram? A mnemonic? Does she want him to guess, or is she giving just enough to obfuscate and throw him, helplessly, awry?

Blumelena. There is nothing.

- who is she? he asks. – does ne1 know?

- She turned up when u were on ur hols, says Moon_fish.

- Mental, says Stokey. Pure mental.

- Why? why iss she mental?

- Back me up, guys, says Stokey.

- LOL, says pris.

- She just comes out with this wierd stuff, says Stokey. – and I'll tell u what else, she doesnt come from B.ham.

- how u no? says pris.

- Just cos, he says.

*

Leo passes another sleepless night. In the morning, grateful for the paling of the sky and the hint of humanity's return, he takes a walk. His head is fuzzy with sedated wakefulness, as though light is distorted, sound focused into a point. As he returns to his house, he collects his post from the hall table, where it's been sitting for days, waiting for the hour when the depression lifted enough to deal with sixteen circulars and bills unnumbered. It's a wad of paper too thick to grasp comfortably in one hand and he thinks that the girl in the flat downstairs is starting to worry; he's seen her poke her head out at the sound of his footfalls on the stairs. He thinks back: this is the first time in six days that he's left his flat.

Blumelena. She's more real to him than the world beyond the screen: a word, a name, a connection. He takes the stairs slowly, head still muzzy, ready for sleep now that the sun is up, sorting through his mail as he goes. A gas bill, a reminder that his overdraft has exceeded the agreed limit. A pamphlet for a wonder cooker, a pizza flyer, a letter from his dentist reminding him that he's overdue a check-up. The envelope is starkly clinical: brown, windowed; franked, not stamped. The name on the front is Devlin, Leonard, and it looks like someone else's name, unrecognisable as his own. Only his mother calls him Leonard.

Devlin, Leonard: due another dental examination. Sorry, sir, I didn't realise you meant me.

*

- I think ur afraid, he says.
- Why? she asks.
- U tell me.
- Why do you think I'm afraid?

He can't say, because you won't tell me your name. He doesn't know pris's name, or Moon_Fish's, or StokeyBoy's. He says – its a feelin I get. R U afraid?

She says – I don't know.

He frowns at the screen.

- maybe u dont want2 talk here. We email?
- No.
- U don't want 2 talk?
- No email.

He's hurt, but he doesn't want her to know it. Instead, he

says,
- what's blumelena? Its drivin me nuts.
- me, she says.
- Is it ur name?
She's silent for a long time. He types in
- hello? U still there?
- something's wrong, she says.
- Computer probs?
- No. I don't know. I just know it's wrong.
- Whats wrong?
- I don't know. Something's happening. I don't know
what it is.
- Don't understand, he says. But it's the wrong thing to
say. He can practically see her recede.
- something's wrong with me, she says.
< Bloom has left the room >
*

A week later, she asks – do u know rain?
- what u mean? he says. He is wary with her; she is
elusive.
- I was just wondering, she says.
He wonders if he should be flippant, if he should break
the tension and write something like – yeah, I no rain, 2 well
<winkyface>. In his fantasy, she writes back – LOL, no wot
u mean. Instead, he says,
- what about rain?
- do u know about it?
He hesitates. His hands hover over the keyboard. He says,
- bloom wot u talkin about, is everything ok?
- nothing, she says. - What did u do 2day?
He says,
– rang up the brew for the hell of it and had a fight. U?
- not much, she says. - The usual.
- What's the usual?
- I don't know, looked out my window. Watched things.
I like to watch
    things.

He's careful. He wants her to keep going, but it's his turn now. He says,

me 2. I go 2 teh park sumtimes 2 c the runners in the morning.

It's nearly true. It's as true as anything else he says.

– why? she asks.

He shrugs. He says,

- bcos they remind me who I am, I thnk. Cos of who I'm not.

- that's a brave answer.

Is it? he thinks.

- r u a brave person? she says.

Again, he asks her – what's up, bloom?

<smileyface> says Bloom. – that's 4 u, lion.

*

He goes to the library. He realises that the idea that information might be available in books that has not yet made it onto the internet is anathema to him, and he wonders, when did that happen? In front of him is a list that he's scrawled on the back of an envelope. It says:

Other languages.

Authors.

Code.

Check encyclopaedias.

Maybe Latin?

It took him all night, after a troubling dream shut out sleep.

He starts with language dictionaries. They have French, Spanish, German, Ancient Greek, Latin, Italian, Japanese. He tries German first because he's convinced it's the most likely. But there is no such word.

*

It gets dark without him noticing. He found an old copy of The Iliad, accidentally-on-purpose and got lost in it about three o'clock, and now the librarian is gently suggesting to the stragglers around him that they might want to pack up their things; the library is closing in five minutes.

Bloom is as elusive as ever. She crouches in the shadows, a dark shape against a dark background, and smiles at him behind her hand. She says, if I wanted you to know, I'd have told you myself. He lifts the envelope, its useless memo on the back a testament to another lost day, flips it over and rolls his eyes. It's the dental reminder: Devlin, Leonard, you have neglected your dental health. It's been looking at him for weeks, goading him, and he's ignored it. Devlin, Leonard couldn't care less.

And then it hits him. It hits him so hard that he almost breaks into a run without realising it, exiting the library so quickly that the librarian decides he's pocketed one of the books, and its not until he pulls up at his garden gate and sparks explode in front of his eyes that he remembers that he hasn't exerted himself beyond a gentle stroll in more than five years.

Devlin, Leonard.

Blum, Elena.

*

His hands hover over the keyboard. He knows that it's a violation. He wishes he could stop himself, but his fingers tap out the letters, his hand glides over the mouse, and he hits search. He gets fifteen good hits, then they get tenuous. Claudia Blum and Elena Schmidt arrived in England in.... [more like this]. Harry and Sylvia Blum... Pennsylvania.... We've just welcomed our latest addition to the family... Elena was born on 07/28/97, weighing 6lb 2oz.... [more like this]. Sponsored links: Buy Blum, Elena online at... He scrolls down, past pop-up ads for credit cards, casinos, personal loans. He finds it near the bottom of the first page, within the top ten: an academic site, but a reference catches his eye: Mortimer Institute of Technology, Birmingham.

Birmingham.

He does another search: Blum Elena AND Birmingham. A dozen sponsored links decide he wants a hotel in Birmingham, Alabama. Only three of the results come up with a reference to Blum, Elena, and top of the page is mortimer.ac.uk. He clicks on the link.

*

At three in the morning, he gives up on sleep and types an email. His fingers are shaking, and when he reads it back he can barely tell the typos from the text, but he clicks send anyway, hazy with recalcitrant wakefulness. Then he shoves a DVD in the machine and waits to pass out on the sofa.

*

Leo's flat is disintegrating. It is sinking daily into decrepitude, and he watches, detached, as though there's a screen in front of his face, filtering the rest of the world into manageable, half-hour slots with breaks every fifteen minutes. He has slipped easily into the middle of the second act, where things start to fall apart in the build-up to the conclusion: a temporary blip that will be resolved before the credits roll. Leo is absolved from the decomposition; there is a piece of the narrative missing, the jigsaw section that makes the picture suddenly take form. The story has apparently swung to the left, and he is waiting for an email to make it swing back to the right.

He watches from the sidelines as pris complains and StokeyBoy vents, as Moon_fish soothes and encourages and secretly burns. pris always notices and she says – hey lion u not talking mayb we smell <winkyface>. When he doesn't respond she sometimes cajoles, sometimes abuses, and sometimes he gives in and says – yeah, tired. Usually he just signs out.

Where is Bloom? Bloom has faded. Bloom has vanished into the ether as

seamlessly as she arrived. He doesn't search for her; what would be the point? His life revolves around the absence of an email, conspicuously not in his inbox.

He reads and re-reads the message that he sent. Each time, the syntax and the three-AM-grammar pierce him with little thorns of humiliation and he knows why he has had no response. He wonders why his life has escaped from him to the point that this is the only thing that matters and, in a rare fit of energy and resolve, he calls up the website again. "Identity as a concept is as ephemeral as ever," it says.

In accepting established notions of the cultural construction of the self, we are, by implication, stating that the concept of I is involuntary and to a large extent shaped without input from the person called myself. The fluidity of Cyberspace further problematizes the issue. Whereas our 'real world' selves are reliant on definitive categories that cannot easily be changed – race, gender, nationality – our Cyberselves are virtual and reliant on our input alone. The fluidity of this environment provides parameters sympathetic to the Turing test of artificial intelligence, and raises intriguing questions. If it is impossible, without conventional markers of identity, to establish definitively the age, gender, nationality or race of a correspondent, how can we determine if, indeed, our companion shares any of our 'real world' characteristics at all?

Professor Elena Blum and her team, intrigued by the dissolution of the self in Cyberspace, are examining the impact of this nascent medium on concepts of identification. In her paper, The Morphology of Identity in the Digital Age, Professor Blum states that:

"In a society marked by cultural disenfranchisement and marginalization, the anonymity of Cyberspace allows the reconstruction of one's identity according to a more satisfactory set of codes. Cyberspace offers the user the chance to alter every aspect of their identifying characteristics, up to and including their genetic code. This clearly has serious implications on our notion of humanity. If something as fundamental as our DNA code can effectively be rewritten within the volatile, shifting boundaries of what we call Cyberspace, might our conception of what we call human not be subject to the same variability?"

Human, thinks Leo, and he looks around his decomposing room.

*

- It doesn't feel right, says Bloom.

He is relieved to hear from her, but afraid to speak. He's afraid she'll disappear again.

Leo says – what doesn't? What's wrong, Bloom?

StokeyBoy says – bloom and lion up a tree. doin thingswe should not see

Leo puts him on ignore.

She is fractured, distracted. He doesn't know how he knows this, but he does. And she has shifted again; now there is no picture of her, only a voice and a shadow. Black on black. She says, I don't know. I'm scared.

Why? What's scaring you?

He's asked her before, and her answer is the same.

- I don't know, Leo. It feels different. Let me ask you something.

- Ask, he says.

- Do you know rain?

Rain again, he thinks, and it still doesn't make sense. He says,

- Bloom, u ask me b4 and I still don't know what u mean, what u mean do u know rain, how can u no rain?

He can hear the pause. He wonders if she is still there, but she is, she hasn't left.

She says – It makes sense to me, I don't know how to make it make sense to you. How do you know rain? I need to know if I know rain.

- you feel it, he says. – Is that wat you mean? U feel it or u c it, then u no its raining.

How can he tell if he's helping? She says – okay, thanks. And then she's gone.

*

Crucial to the construction will be the entity's conception of itself. Just as an amnesia-sufferer may theoretically adopt a life entirely at variance with their life prior to memory loss, it is clear that identity-construction is closely linked to our remembrance of stories told to ourselves about ourselves. Therefore, it is conceivable that an entity with the capacity to pass the Turing test may well be unaware that theirs is an artificially constructed intelligence. This clearly raises a number of ethical questions, not least the legitimacy of deluding an intelligence with the capacity of self-awareness as to its construction of self.

*

He just wants an email. He wants her to respond, to tell him he's a nutcase and he needs to get a life. He just wants someone else to tell him.

Leo has taken to checking his inbox fifty, sixty times a day. He opens it up and watches it, willing her to write. He compulsively clicks refresh, waits – ten, twenty, thirty – refresh. Nothing. Click – refresh. Nothing. White page. Please sign in again. Hope flares; tiny, infinitesimal hope, and he signs back in, clicks refresh once, twice, just to be sure.

Nothing. He is a crazy man, waiting to be told he's crazy.

Click – refresh. Nothing. Silence.

*

He says – bloom tell me about u.

She says – what do you want me to tell you?

- tell me about what u see out of your window.

- I see life going by, she says.

- What do u see? Do u c people? What do u look at?

- I see everything going just as it ought to be. I don't know why it scares me. I don't know why it's wrong.

Don't be scared, he wants to tell her, but there is no way to explain.

*

How, therefore, are we to identify a set of human rights for a non-human entity? Is it akin to denying the fact of an adoption to an adopted child? Might we not make the same arguments for the adoptee's sense of self, constructed as it is by the identities of those whom the child believes are its parents? If the impact on an adoptee's sense of self may be catastrophic, might not the impact of a discovery by a sentient, self-aware, non-human entity that its origins are synthetic be significantly more so?

*

On the nineteenth day of his confinement, Leo leaves his flat. In the post-dawn grey, he walks to the little corner store on the other side of the park, where everything costs three times as much, but he doesn't think he can face the neon lights and cavern-acoustics of the supermarket. On the way home, fuzzy and disjointed, he rests for a moment on a damp wooden bench and watches his partners in wakefulness as they pass by: joggers, night-shift workers, early risers. He searches for them a hint of familiarity, an indication that they share some tiny piece of common ground, but they are blank, impenetrable. Strangers.

It starts to rain.

*

- How do you define yourself? asks Bloom.
- That's a good question, he says.
- Give me a brave answer.

He hesitates, and is forced to admit that there are no brave answers.

He says,

– I am the sum of my experiences. I am what I've learned.

– But what is that?

- I've learned what I like and don't like, he says.

- Tell me what you don't like.

He says, because it's the first thing that comes to mind,

– I don't like custard.

– How do you know that?

- Because I ate custard and I didn't like it.

- You are what you've learned. You are a person who doesn't like custard.

- I am a person who likes my own company. I am a person who likes to read. I am a person who would rather sit alone and read a book at lunch than join in a boring conversation. I am a person who likes music, but certain types of music. I am a person who either likes something a lot or doesn't like it at all.

Who are you? he wants to ask. So he does. She says,

I don't know if I like custard.

He knows that he doesn't need Elena Blum to write back for him to be certain. He's known that for a while now.

*

Reality is fluid within Cyberspace. It is also subjective. To such an entity, reality within these boundaries must be as convincing as that which is provided to us by our own five senses. After all, what is 'reality', other than a series of coded messages interpreted subjectively by electrical signals within our brains? Barring interaction with the 'outside' world that is not within a series of strictly defined parameters, it is conceivable that our hypothetical entity may remain in a state of ignorance as to our alternate levels of existence. This is to be desired. Exposure to the fact of its origin may, as we have seen, be catastrophic to the entity's sense of self. The effects of this cannot be predicted.

*

He wonders where she found out about rain. He wants to tell her, it's all right, don't think about it if it worries you. He wants to make it better, in a little way. Maybe if he made it better in a little way, it would be better for him, because he so wanted it not to be true. He so wanted his only connection in a life of fibre optic cables and fluid, shifting selves to have been real.

She says,

– so then I realised that I was aware of the rain, and that if I was aware of it, I must be feeling it. I must be seeing it. So that's all right, isn't it?

- Yes, he tells her. That's all right. You know rain.

He doesn't know where her sense of malaise has come from, or how the seeds of doubt came to be planted in her fertile, fluid, shifting self. He only knows that if it's making her unhappy, then that's something that can be dealt with.

He says,
- I'm glad we met, Bloom.
- Me too, she says.
*

This is, of course, an entirely hypothetical argument. The tools for further exploration may exist at some point in the future, but for now our entity must remain an academic postulation.
*

- Time for me to hit the hay, he tells her. – I'm up early in the morning.
- Talk to you tomorrow?
- I'll be here, same time. Goodnight, Bloom.
- Goodnight, Leo.
< Leo has left the room >

Edited by Sam Taylor

FRUIT OF MEMORY
By Daniel Z Klein

She left ten months ago.

I would have told you, back then, that I had no clue it was coming. That it hit me from out of nowhere. That she was volatile. But of course, the way these things go, I look back now and I analyse what I know now, and I see the signs everywhere. Suddenly, every word she said flashes neon red with warning. Hindsight is my favourite drug; it's a real mind enhancer.

And of course I do not know if she said these words exactly as I recall, or if my memory edited what happened then to make more sense. Maybe my mind wanted to see signals in what she said in hindsight, maybe I wanted everything to make more sense, and maybe my mind adjusted its recording of those days and inserted the signs I now see. I will never know.

Here is what I know for sure: on the last night that she shared my bed, we were both drunk. It was a miserable night. I had gotten into a fight with an old friend not knowing why. Today, of course, I see that the friction between me and my wife was too much to take for me, that I had to lash out at someone. My friend was simply in the wrong place at the wrong time.

And maybe this, too, is an edit; maybe I was actually upset with him. I remember bringing up things that he had said to me before I even met my wife. Perhaps these complaints had lived in me for as long as I had known him, perhaps my frustration did nothing more than overpower my love for the man and bring these complaints to the forefront.

You have to forgive my paranoia. It is an occupational hazard. When one works quite closely with human memory, one learns not to trust it. One learns that nearly anything is better than memory. In one experiment that we organized we coupled a memorization exercise with emotional trauma—and it should have been a warning sign, I see now, how much I enjoyed designing an experiment that triggered emotional trauma in my subjects—and showed that given very specific circumstances, blind guessing often outperforms recall. When you can demonstrate statistically that people are better off guessing than trying to remember, you lose some faith in memory.

Memory is a coping mechanism. We all grow old, we all miss opportunities, we all carry regrets and anxieties. Memory helps us cope. Memory stimulates happiness in a very specific way (we refer to it as nostalgia, but that is only part of the story), memory rearranges the past so that it makes sense. Memory makes heroes of us all. Remember how smart you were in school? How brilliant you were as a young child? Remember the physical feats of your youth or the brilliant brainwaves of your early 20s? Chances are, none of these things happened anywhere near the way you remember them. Yes, the emotions at the core are real. You were really proud of your achievements. Only that you had a different scope for what an achievement was back then, and now that this scope has changed, the achievements have to change to match. Your memory strategically lies to you to keep you happy.

This is a good thing. If our memory was without flaw, if we recorded every instant of our lives like so many walking CCTV cameras, the human race would not have made it to this point. We would have collectively offed ourselves thousands of years ago.

Memory is a coping mechanism.

The last night my wife shared my bed, we were both drunk and miserable. I tried to make love to her, but I could not maintain my erection and she could not maintain her interest. We drifted off and fell asleep. I woke up in the middle of the night, still drunk rather than hungover, angry now rather than miserable, and we tried again, and something happened.

Now if I were to tell you this story from unaided memory,

ten months after the fact, I would not believe a word of it. I would know, for a fact, that my memory was overstating my achievement, that I probably fucked her adequately and we were both relieved and happy and that was that. But I am not telling you this story from unaided memory. I am telling you this story based on the first memberry created for non-academic purposes. I am telling you the story that is—was, as of ten minutes ago—enshrined in the first recreational memberry.

I work in accelerated learning. It started with memory supplements and mental performance boosters, but when we learned how to trigger neuron activation cascades very accurately, someone asked the question of what would happen if we could record the neuron activation cascade associated with a specific memory and then recreate it. What if we gave you the memory of studying for 20 hours? Would you learn? Even a little bit?

We tried it on rats. We had a rat learn a labyrinth, then hooked it up to the memory extractor and stimulated the memory again and again, until the bots picked up the full NAC.

The first thing we discovered was that we were quite good at making rats forget how to navigate a labyrinth: the original host would lose the knowledge of the labyrinth after the extraction process. There's a bunch of theories here, but we never looked too closely into it. We figured that if the knowledge was lost on extraction, it wouldn't be too bad: after all, we would then be able to reproduce the knowledge as many times as we liked and even reintroduce it to the original host.

As it turned out it wasn't that easy.

Rats who received the memory would instantly learn the labyrinth. The results were so clear we practically popped the champagne already. This was it, we thought. We had finally revolutionized learning!

And then we came back to the lab the next day. No, the rats weren't dead—that would have been too easy. They had simply forgotten all about the labyrinth. They had to relearn it from scratch. We explained it away: that without self-reflection the memory couldn't take hold, that their brains were too simple to learn long-term from a memory, and so on. We explained it away because we didn't want to believe the data.

We pushed on. Pigs, dogs, monkeys. Always the same results: the memory, when freshly inserted, seemed to do what we hoped it would do, but without fail the learning effect would go away within twenty-four hours.

How we were able to move on to human test subjects so quickly is a subject I will leave for the inevitable tell-all shockumentary: "Inside the academic drug lab". Yes, we should have been more careful, no, we shouldn't have lied as much to get our requests processed by the Food and Drug Administration, and no, we shouldn't have ignored all the red flags we did ignore. The rats went crazy for the memory pills. There were clear signs of habit-forming effects, but we ignored everything that didn't help us push the product forward. We hadn't had a single success story and we really needed one.

The first human memberry was harvested from my mind. I memorized a set of 50 obscure Turkish words. The extraction was a gruelling process; we tried it under sedation and it didn't seem to work at all. Today we know that the memory needs to flash before your eyes for the extraction to take hold. The extraction machinery's electronic impulses stimulated the memory playback over and over. Things became hazy as the intensely boring hour I spent memorizing strings of letters flashed before my eyes again and again. I noticed the memory starting to change even as it was being extracted.

Jerome took the first memberry. Today I know how intimate an action this is, to live through the memory of another man. Today I would feel dirty.

Of course, they weren't called memberries back then. This was before the multi-droplet synthfoam delivery system that reminded us of drupelets in fruits like blackberries.

Here is what happens when you ingest a memberry: the memory assembles itself in your brain in waves and flashes of imagery, not necessarily in chronological order, coming to you in sudden onset sensations that echo and fade and return. Eventually you reach a critical mass of stimulant and the entire neuron activation cascade locks in place and plays out sequentially.

Here is what it feels like when you ingest a memberry: incredible. Thrilling. Exciting. Intoxicating. You are having a waking dream. It's a trip. Quite literally a trip. Serotonin and various endorphins are released. And on a pure entertainment level, it is the most immersive form of narrative consumption we know. You literally live another person's experiences.

My first berry was flawed in many, many ways. Worst of all, we did not change scenery or let sufficient time pass between the target memory and the extraction process, so that my immense anxiety over the safety of the extraction machinery bled back heavily into the memory, to the point where Jerome described that he remembered studying these Turkish words in a constant state of panic, feeling the sweat run down his forehead, his heart beating in his chest.

Jerome became obsessed with this aspect of the process and went back to the memory, growing berry after berry from the mother berry of my memory. We had never known him like this. Jerome had always been a diligent researcher, but he was the most level-headed one of us. He was the one we had to convince to cheat the FDA process to skip forward to human testing. And yet he kept going back time and again, taking notes of how the memory morphed each time, until the physiological states he described in his notes started manifesting. He would come out of the memory sweating, shaking, palpitating. When he started to scream upon surfacing we asked him to stop. He said not to worry, that he barely remembered the discomfort the next day.

But the results weren't what we wanted them to be, and we were starting to worry about more than just Jerome's well-being. We were slowly coming out of the heady rush of what seemed like a major breakthrough. Berry memories weren't taking. They were fleeting, like dreams, especially susceptible to sleep. So we decided to lock the mother berry away. In retrospect I think we had a hypothesis about what the frequent trips were doing to Jerome, but we couldn't quite admit it to ourselves, so we experimented on our co-worker. At the time, of course, it was only security concerns that made us lock the foamy egg-shaped template away. Without the mother berry, Jerome could grow no further ingestible memberries of my memory.

More than anything else I remember the sinking feeling in the pit of my stomach when we came to the lab the next week to find the entire place trashed. Drawers torn from worktops and thrown across the room, cupboards smashed in and toppled, desks turned upside down and pried open. And in the middle of it all, Jerome, crowbar in hand, breathing heavily, sweat and blood on his forehead. When we entered the room his eyes locked on us—reddened, pupils extremely constricted as though he had developed a sudden sensitivity to light—and he screamed at us. He didn't actually say anything, he just produced a guttural grunt followed by an inhuman hissing sound.

Then he tried to bite me.

We learned that when he couldn't find the mother berry extracted from my memory of memorizing the Turkish words, he grew a berry from the only other mother berry he could get his hands on—that original rat berry in which the memory of the rat navigating the labyrinth was saved. Into which had bled the pure animal fright the rat had of the extraction machinery. The lack of understanding, the panic, the pain, filtered through a mind dominated entirely by fight or flight reflexes and animal savagery.

When he ate the rat berry, something in his brain disconnected, and I'm sad to say it never fully reconnected. We restrained him, eventually, and after going through withdrawal for a few days he was mostly fine. But from that time on he was never able to concentrate on work for more than a few minutes. He would get up and look for food, or drink all kinds of stimulating beverages, or go to the bathroom. The latter he would do with worrying frequency, to the point that we asked him if he was alright. His answers still sounded entirely human, but there was an odd aspect to how harshly he delivered them, how quickly he jumped from one mood to another. He informed us that he went to the bathroom so often in order to masturbate. He said this without any shame whatsoever, and as a matter of fact he soon started touching himself at his desk. That was when we sent him to a psychiatrist, who diagnosed him with a psychotic break of some sort.

He left the institute. When he was gone it was as though we had exorcized some evil spirit, as though all the horrible things that had befallen him had never really happened. We wrote up our experiments on monkeys properly, got a paper or two published, applied for and received more grant money. We were waiting, stalling for time, unsure what to do next.

I saw him once. At least I'm pretty sure I saw him. Maybe I just put his face onto a random homeless person so that I could properly feel guilty about the whole episode. I'm sure I saw him though, fighting with an old man in very soiled clothing in front of a super market. The security guard broke up the fight and sent them both away, and I could swear the man who looked like Jerome hissed at him.

Fast forward to ten months ago, when my wife left me. I guess I should finally finish telling you what happened that morning.

We had sex. Something clicked. Something worked. Things came together the way they normally didn't. I know that at first she was indulging me, half-asleep as she was, and I was struck by a sudden fear (I remember the fear sharply, the sudden cold, the pumping of blood, the dizziness) as some animal part of my brain made a connection that my consciousness would need some time to arrive at. My reptile hind-brain knew that she was ending it hours before my highly evolved human fore-brain did. And that fear drove me on to heretofore unknown heights of performance and pleasure. Something changed about the way I moved, the way we moved, and I saw in her face how indulgence turned to sudden surprise and then there was nothing but pleasure in her expression.

We made love for hours. I remember seeing the sun come up half-way through, and then going on even longer, with short blackouts in between. This is not something we had ever done; not on our first night together, not at any point during our honeymoon, and certainly not on our wedding night. I saw an adoration in her eyes for me, I saw a passion I had not ever seen in her, and she showed me a side of herself that was new to me as well. During the entire time we did not say a word. We made plenty of sounds, but they were guttural, animal sounds; expressive enough, but non-verbalized.

And like I said in the beginning, I would not trust this story if I was retelling it from unaided memory. But I'm not.

When we finally surfaced from our fever dream of passion, I heated up some leftovers and we talked over food. She told me how she had felt trapped for so long now, how I was being passive aggressive even in my indulgences, even when I did give her her freedom, and part of me thought, but I just fucked you! For so very long! And you enjoyed it, you enjoyed it so much! Why are we doing this? Why are we ending this?

And of course that is the most irrational thought in the world. I still felt intoxicated by the memory, but the first details were beginning to fade. The idea came to me when I realized that I didn't know for sure, who had spoken first after we were done. I decided not to allow this memory to slip away. I decided to enshrine it forever, to encase it in a foamy soft prison from whence it would never be able to flee.

It must have been obvious that my attention wasn't with my wife anymore. She became angry. I'm not listening to her, she said, and this is important. Yes, I said, it is important.

We're breaking up, I said, we're getting a divorce. She was taken aback by my sudden bluntness, but when she recovered she said yes, we were. I said that it would probably be best if she were to leave now. So I could think about this. She touched my hand and said she was so sorry it had to end this way. I smiled at her and told her I wasn't.

When she had left I jumped into my car and ran all the red lights on the way to the institute. Yes, we should have destroyed the human-compatible machine, as the institute instructed us to. Yes, we had agreed not to use the machine for further human testing until we had refined the process to the point that we could be certain it was safe, the point where we could be sure there wouldn't be another Jerome, but this was an emergency. The most magical moment of my life was slipping away, a moment of such transcendent poignancy, such bitter-sweet contrast and so much pleasure. For all of human history we had been slaves to the slow decay of memory. Artists fought it when they recorded their memories in paintings or texts, but the conscious process was always an alteration. This was pure and simple extraction.

I extracted the memory. I felt strangely relieved when I realized it was gone from my mind. There was some bleed-over with the dinner we had afterwards. Some of that was gone too, and that felt good as well. But I had managed to do what I set out to do. I slotted the still-warm mother berry into the incubator and immediately grew a berry. The process was much more elaborate now, with the individual nano-bot collectives responsible for major sub-points of the neuron activation cascade locked away in separate droplets, the whole fruit consisting of dozens of these droplets. It was more robust this way, more reliable. You put the berry in your mouth and your saliva would slowly dissolve droplet after droplet, slowly releasing the different layers of the memory, affording your brain time to adjust.

I put the first berry in my mouth and bit down hard. The memory came all at once: first the orgasms, squeezed all into a single instant, then all her facial expressions, the sounds, the smells, the cramps, the euphoria, and slowly the moments separated and arranged themselves chronologically. And once they were all in place, once the memory was locked, the full neuron activation cascade played out, the entire scene running in front of my eyes in a few minutes. Every taste, every thrust, every grunt.

Even before the memory was over I knew I would need more. This wasn't just some cheap trip; this was personal, this was wonderful, this was almost romantic: a shrine to my love for her.

I took the incubator with me, set it up in my now-empty home. I stole as much of the feedstock as I could. And of course the rest of the group immediately knew what had happened. I called in sick the next day, and the day after that, depleting the rawberries with frightening speed. When I did appear at work again, my colleagues were waiting for me, chairs arranged in a semi-circle, as in some cheap soap opera version of an intervention. Return the apparatus to the institute, they said, and no one will have to know what you did. We can help you, they said. Like we helped Jerome, I asked, and they had no answer.

I ordered as much feedstock as I could, through the institute, burning a sizeable chunk of our grant on it. I invented some pretext to have it delivered straight to my house.

They threatened me at the institute, of course, but since we weren't even supposed to have the human-compatible machinery anymore after the Jerome incident they could hardly come after me with the police. Help, officer, this man has stolen our highly illegal machinery and we want it back! All they could do in the end was have me fired, which served me well as I didn't want to go back anyway.

In hindsight, this was a little short-sighted.

Months passed. My savings and my feedstock dwindled. I remember the day I went through all my credit cards at the supermarket trying to buy a cart full of frozen pizza and not one of the cards would work. The humiliation was exquisite and my first thought was that I should extract and imprint this memory too, to record this peak of sensation, even though it was a very negative sensation.

Hunger is a wonderful motivator. I half expected to see Jerome at the soup kitchen, but again that would have been too easy. Instead I got my free soup and walked out, thinking about where I could stash away the incubator and the leftover feedstock when I inevitably lost the house.

I was approached by a man who looked like an old, homeless veteran. I remember feeling apprehensive. I don't like beggars. It angers me that they have the power to make me feel guilty. He mumbled something at me, and at first I didn't understand and said "sorry", to indicate that I didn't have any spare change, and for once I really didn't. But then he repeated himself and I realized he was trying to sell me drugs. I laughed. If only you knew, I said, if only you knew the thing that I have! What drug could possibly compete with that! He fixed me in his eyes, an intelligence I hadn't expected shining through, and asked me what I meant.

I should have kept on walking. I should have sold my computer for another month's worth of food. I should have figured out a hiding place for the incubator and the feedstock and accepted that I would lose my house. Instead I saw a way out and I took it.

He was extremely suspicious when I showed him his first berry, but I could see in his eyes that he had a true entrepreneur's instincts. He realized I really had something better than whatever he was selling, and he realized I was desperate enough to sell through him. He would be able to milk me and my drug.

So I gave him a berry. I gave him the memory of me sleeping with my wife for the last time, for what seemed like an eternity, through undreamt-of peaks of pleasure and lust. It was spiced with the bleedback of my extreme anxiety during the talk over food that followed it. I had accidentally created the perfect berry. Lust, pleasure, anxiety, stress, exertion, exhaustion, happiness, desperation. All the prime factors that release that tasty cocktail of homebrew drugs our brain is so stingy with most of the time.

When he emerged from the memory with a wet spot spreading quickly on his trousers he only asked me how many I had of these and how quickly I could make them. I told him of the limited feedstock and how the special nano-bot substrate was currently available only through academic channels, but he waved that off. He knew people, he implied, that could procure what needed procuring. How quickly was all he wanted to know. I told him very quickly. Given the feedstock, water and electricity I could produce berries much more quickly than he could possibly sell them.

I was wrong with that prediction. Turns out there is an untapped market for pleasurable memory stimulation. And it also turns out that the ephemeral nature of the memories implanted by memberries makes them the stuff of a drug dealer's wet dreams: highly stimulating, highly habit-forming, low on long-term satisfaction.

I watched the sensationalist news reports with a keen interest and a little bit of guilt, but it seemed the progress we had made at the institute since the Jerome incident had paid off. As long as the memory was absorbed in a slow, controlled manner, the stuff was dangerous and habit-forming, but not deadly, not life-threatening in any fashion. It also helped not to eat crazed rat-berries. So when the press finally got their hands on a memberry junkie with a psychotic break, they leaped on the story like the misery junkies they are. I assumed it would be a patient with a previous history of mental illness, someone who would have broken one way or another. I could not see at this point how a berry could break someone's mind.

Until, of course, I watched the report and saw the patient in her restraints, struggling against the leather straps around her wrists and ankles, screaming "no no no" over and over. They described how she was found in her house by herself with all reflective surfaces smashed in or scratched and a large stash of berries on her dining room table. I saw the picture of the table and realized instantly that the arrangement of pots and plates and glasses was non-random. Yes, everything was filled with berries rather than actual food, but I recognized the arrangement instantly. My wife had recreated the table I had set for us on that last day, the memory of it having bled into the berry. I cannot imagine what she must have felt going through the memory from my perspective a hundred times, seeing herself fucking herself, feeling me feeling her, thinking through my fucked up mind my fucked up thoughts about herself, to the point where the identities of real-she and berry-she clashed and annihilated each other. It makes sense that she could not stand to see her reflection anymore, as the separation between real-she and mirror-she must have felt like the reflection between real and berry. But that was not enough and, as the reporter told the camera breathlessly, they had to restrain her when she tried to scratch out her own eyes.

I destroyed the mother berry. I originally designed the synthetic neuron equivalents inside the mother berry, the minibrain that lives through the memory every time a berry is incubated, but it still surprised me when the nutrient-rich fluid that leaked out of the cut-up mother berry looked so much like blood. It is dead now, anyway, and no further berries can be grown from it. I called my partner immediately and informed him that I had withdrawn from our joint venture. I'm not sure what I expected, but I thought at least if I was honest to him... well.

He told me not to go anywhere and that he was coming over. To talk about it, he said. I said there was nothing to talk about. The mother berry was dead. End of story. He barely controlled his rage, but still said he would need to come over. Settle accounts.

I expect they will threaten me, perhaps even torture me, find some kind of way to get me to restart berry production. They don't understand that no matter what, they will never have a berry like this again. The mother is gone. The big one, the perfect storm. Maybe they can find a colleague of mine from the institute days, maybe they can force them to explain how the extraction process works. But they would have to construct a memory first.

Not just any memory. I don't know what it was that made my berry so addictive, but I'd guess it was the combination of pain and pleasure, of animal fright and complete abandon to lust. You do not make a perfect storm; you come upon one, and if you understand what just happened, you record it.

I can hear a car pulling up outside. What would I do, in his shoes? Clearly this was an unprecedented gold streak. My understanding is that he scaled up his operation considerably, that turf wars were fought and won over the product. The economics of drug dealing will not allow my partner to back down, I am now realizing. No, he will be forced to try and recapture that first berry. He will have to put a host through the whole range of feelings I felt. There are crude ways to make a human subject feel pain and pleasure. It is also possible to induce emotional trauma. Remember those experiments I talked about in the beginning? It is possible, and with all the incentives to get it right and no oversight whatsoever, many of these subjects will remain scarred for life.

Eventually, there will be another berry. They will get it wrong. They will have to try again, and again. The novelty of these lesser berries will fade more rapidly, but once they have figured out the extraction process, what's to stop them from trying very many times, bringing their hosts to ever-new heights of trauma and stimulation, flooding the market with new berries. And when they can't get the cocktail of trauma and emotion right, they will probably turn to darker and darker subject matters, hoping those will make up for what these berries will lack in emotional impact.

They're at my door now. There is a kitchen knife in my hand. Maybe I will use it. Maybe I will end this, before it gets worse. Of course I won't: I've always been a coward. They won't have to threaten me much. I will go along with whatever they will do. Whatever it takes to create the next berry. And when they're through with me, they'll find others. There will always be others.

Edited by Sam Taylor

ARTIFACT
By John Gribbin

"We've got some more data on The Artifact."

The Director looked up from his screen, the automatic complaint about being interrupted without warning stifled in his throat. The Artifact. Even when Gallucci spoke the name, you could tell it had capital letters. The most important discovery in the history of humankind – an alien artifact moving, painfully slowly, in to the Solar System. It seemed to be in free fall, which meant months would elapse before the Orion probe could intercept it, even with gravity assist at Jupiter.

"It's not alien."

That really did get the Director's attention.

"Pause," he instructed the computer, scarcely hearing its acknowledgement, and waited for Gallucci to explain. The woman, standing there with an expression like the cat that got the cream, might like drama – a trait he blamed on her Italian ancestry – but she must have good data to back up such a claim.

"It's definitely following the reverse of the Pioneer 10 trajectory. I've got some more figures from the archive. It's even speeding up slightly faster than if it were in free fall, but at an exponentially increasing rate. And," she paused for effect, but the Director didn't rise to the bait. She'd continue in her own good time. Gallucci glanced at the pad she was holding. "And, I've established that this exactly matches the unexplained deceleration of Pioneer 10 measured back in the twentieth century!"

"Is that all?" He was disappointed. "Just more evidence that whoever sent the probe picked up Pioneer 10 and is letting us know about it gently. Giving us time to adjust to their existence."

She shook her head. "No, no. It's an artifact, all right, but it's not an alien artifact. We've managed to interrogate it. It's ours. Well, NASA's. It is Pioneer 10."

"How did you – " he stopped himself. He didn't need the technicalities, and he probably wouldn't understand them. Administration had long since atrophied his brain. The stuff they were doing with the Deep Space Array certainly matched Clarke's definition of magic. Six dishes at the vertices of a hexagon, parked at Jupiter's L3 point and working as one, feeding data back by laser.

"How," he started again, "could it be coming back? Unless someone turned it around?"

"Not someone; something. A phenomenon." She smiled. Now she had his full attention.

"We've matched the exponential decrease in the velocity of Pioneer 10 going out and the exponential increase in the velocity of what we now know to be Pioneer 10 coming in. They correspond to a reflection – there's a cusp of some kind, just beyond the Oort Cloud. Rikky did the number-crunching. It isn't Little Green Men catching the craft and throwing it back at us, it must have slowed down to a stop then started back the way it came. Exactly the way it came."

He shook his head. A cusp? He tried to picture it. An image of his skateboarding son came into his head. Shooting up the half-pipe, slowing all the while, then shooting back down again the way he had come, getting faster all the time.

"You mean it hit a wall?"

"Well, bounced off a wall, more like."

"A wall around the Solar System?"

"I prefer to think of it as a kind of horizon, a kind of event horizon. My guess is it lets stuff in, but it won't let stuff out, as far as we can tell."

"Like a black hole?"

"Sort of. But without the singularity."

"That means new physics."

"You got it." Gallucci's smile widened. "Can we publish, Boss?"

"Not so fast." Of course they had to publish. But what were the implications?

"What are the implications?"

She shrugged. Clearly, the implications didn't bother her. What mattered was the discovery.

"Oh, I guess there are two possibilities. At least, Rikky and I couldn't think of any more.

"One." She held up a finger. "The horizon, or wall, is artificial. The zoo hypothesis is right. Someone has walled off the Solar System to stop us contaminating the rest of the Universe. So we have found evidence of alien intelligence after all. Although they might have gone away by now. No telling when the wall was built.

"Two." She raised the next digit. "It could be natural. There is no outside. Everything beyond the cusp is an illusion – some kind of projection which we interpret as stars and galaxies and stuff.

"Of course," she paused for a moment as if another thought had just hit her. "You could combine both hypotheses. An artificial horizon through which we are deliberately being fed pretty pictures of a virtual universe. We might be in a zoo, but whoever put us here wants to keep us amused, perhaps to stop us finding out the truth. Could explain why every time we think we have a good explanation of the Universe, like the old Big Bang theory, or the Weizmann Model, new observations come along to confuse the picture."

"And if you publish, they'll know that we have found out. What happens then?"

"Haven't thought of that," she replied. "But I bet it will be interesting."

ORIENTATION
By C M Martin

He was in Hell.

He wasn't quite sure how he'd gotten there. There had been no judgment at the throne of God, no interview with St. Peter at the Pearly Gates, none of the customary formalities that the nuns in his long-ago Catholic schooldays had told him about. The last thing he could remember was that night at the hospital, with all his relatives gathered around him like football fans around a giant plasma screen TV. He must have blacked out, and now he was in Hell.

He wasn't even sure how he knew this was Hell. There were no flames, no demons trapped in pits of brimstone, writhing and shrieking as their flesh melted from their bones only to grow back and melt again. There was nothing here but a simple office containing a desk, a few chairs, and dozens upon dozens of very tall file cabinets that lined the walls. But despite the lack of evidence, he knew, deep within himself, that through some terrible macabre mistake, he was now in Hell.

"NEXT!"

He jumped. Sitting behind the desk was a woman, or at least he thought that was what she was supposed to be. He couldn't imagine how he'd missed seeing her before. Perhaps she hadn't been there before. She looked a little like a refrigerator with a blonde wig and a mouthful of shark's teeth, and she had the voice of a bullfrog with a mouth full of gravel. Her one bright purple eye was staring straight at him.

"I said NEXT, puke-puss! You think I got all eternity to wait for you to pull your head outta your crack? Now SIDDOWN!" She pointed at the chair in front of the desk.

Dazed, he dropped into the chair and stared blankly at her. She pulled out a legal pad and a red pen.

"Name?"

"What?"

"Your name, ass-wipe! You do have one, don't you? What did the nurse at the free clinic call you when you came in for your shots?"

"Ummm... Donald, Donald O'Grady. But look. This has got to be some kind of..."

"Yeah, yeah. I know the sob stories. You don't belong here, there's been a screw-up in the paperwork; you have a guaranteed reservation for the resort up top. I've heard 'em all a billion times, and frankly, you wad of crotch fungus, I ain't interested. The Boss says you're a new resident, and that's all I need to know."

"The...the Boss?" He swallowed hard, noticing for the first time just how thirsty he was. "You...you don't mean..."

"Well, I ain't shitting out eggs for the Easter Bunny, booger-brain. Let's get this over with. The sooner you're processed, the sooner I can quit listening to you whine." She got up and headed for one of the file cabinets. Muttering something under her breath, she began to rise towards the ceiling as he watched, fascinated and more than a little nauseated by the sight. She wasn't wearing any underwear. She floated to the level of the very top drawer, at least 30 feet from the floor, yanked it open, and began to dig through some files with all the enthusiasm of a monkey picking lice. In a minute or two, she floated back down holding a rather skinny tan folder.

"Here we go," she said. "Donald O'Grady. Caucasian, American, Catholic. What a fucking loaf of white bread you are, pus-boy. Date of birth, September 17th, 1945. Date of death... "she turned to look at the calendar on the wall behind her, or rather her head turned 180 degrees, while her massive body stayed firmly planted. Donald screamed.

The head whirled back around. "What are you pissing your pants for now? Oh, the head trick." She laughed raucously. "A little something I picked up from some movie. Great bit, huh?"

"Look," he tried again, "I know I don't belong here. I

was a good Catholic! I was an altar boy, for Christ's sake!"

A piece of the ceiling fell on his head. "Ouch!" he cried, rubbing at the lump that was already growing.

"Watch your mouth," she snapped. "We don't use the C word down here, dick breath. The Boss ain't too fond of it. As for your precious holy fucked-up life, I've got the record right here." She flipped through the folder. "March 12th, 1968. A Friday during Lent. You ate three, count 'em, three cheeseburgers, altar boy. Had yourself a regular little cow orgy, and you forgot to confess it. No absolution, no forgiveness. You should have turned Baptist. They can't drink or fuck, but they can eat all the meat their colons can handle. You blew it big-time with your oh-so forgiving Savior," she sneered.

"But... but, if that's all that's on my record, I should be in Purgatory," he protested. "I know my rights."

She laughed again, tongue lolling out of her mouth as she snorted and sprayed spittle all over the desk, his file, and him. "Purgatory!" she finally choked out. "You Catholics are the dumbest sons of bitches ever to walk the planet. Just because some saint said it 800 years ago, you think it's carved in a fucking rock! Well, I got news for you. We closed Purgatory down more than 100 years ago. Budget cuts, you know. No profit in it, and the Boss got tired of warehousing all those mealy-mouthed, lukewarm fools while their relatives prayed and whined to the Other One to get them sprung. Nope, you're right where you put yourself, and no amount of prayers, priests, or pissing around is gonna get you out." Digging in a drawer, she handed him a brass key. "Here you go, room two million, one hundred and seventy thousand, four hundred and ten. Go right through this door and down the hall a couple hundred miles. I hope you're wearing your Nikes, you pussy. There's one set of sheets on the bed and two towels in the john, but you'd better keep them clean; room service isn't scheduled for your wing for another 689 years. Oh, and keep the noise down if you know what's good for you. The Cleveland Axe Maniac is next door. Fun guy, but he's still got a shitter of a migraine from the electric chair."

"Wait!" Donald cried desperately.

"What now?" She snapped. "You think I got no one to process today but you, shit-face? Beelzebub's balls, they're stacked up in reception like hookers at the Vegas Airport."

"I want to see your boss," he said. "This has got to be a mistake, and I'm going to set it right. I demand you take me to him!"

"Ooooooh, ain't you the brave one? Well, all right. It's no ham slice off my ass, buddy. I'll see if the Boss is free." She picked up a cordless phone (red, he noticed) and punched in a number.

"Boss? I got a new one here. Donald O'Grady. Yeah, that's the one. Little worm is bitching he got the shaft. Wants to see you. Can I bring him down? O.K." She dropped the phone on the floor. It whimpered and crawled back up onto the desk, quivering slightly. "Come on, you little bag of snot. I hope you appreciate this." She marched him through the door at the rear of the office.

They were in a long, wide hallway lined with doors. Every door was closed, but Donald could just imagine the torments that were hidden inside: lakes of fire, demons poking at sinners with pitchforks, people being force-fed brimstone and molten lava. He shuddered. How could this have happened? If I get out of this, I'll take holy orders, he vowed to himself. I'll work with lepers. I'll never eat meat again.

"Here we are." His guide stopped in front of a red door with a brass plate that simply read THE BOSS. "You're on your own from here, flea dick." She stomped off in the direction they had come.

Donald stood outside the door for a long moment. His bravado was gone. But what choice did he have? "It's this or the Cleveland Axe Maniac," he said to himself. He knocked.

"Come in," a cheerful voice called. Donald opened the door, stepped inside, and stopped, in shock.

It was another office, larger than the first and tastefully decorated in crimson brocade and rich oak paneling. Sitting behind an enormous desk was a neatly dressed man in a pinstripe suit. His middle was a little soft, his hair a little thin. He looked like... Donald.

"Come on in," he smiled. "You must be Donald."

Donald edged into the room, still staring at his double. "You're.....Satan?" His voice was barely a squeak.

"Actually, the name is Lucifer, but whatever."

"You...you look like..." he couldn't get the words out.

"Oh, get a grip, man. It makes perfect sense, if you only stop to think about it. He created Man in His image; Man creates me in his image. I look a little different to everyone. Can I get you a drink?"

Donald dropped into one of the leather client chairs in front of the desk. "Yes, thank you," he said feebly. "A drink would be very nice."

Lucifer rose and went to a small refrigerator built into one wall. "I've got cola, tomato juice, Dr Pepper, and beer," he said. "What's your pleasure?"

"Christ, I'd love a beer. Ouch!" Another chunk of plaster bounced off his head.

"Watch your mouth." Lucifer handed him a cold tallboy, which he downed in two long gulps.

"Ah, that's better. Look, none of this is what I expected. And that secretary..."

The Devil waved a negligent hand. "No problem. Everyone's a bit rattled at first. And don't pay any attention to Selma. She's a pathological liar and the biggest bitch in the universe."

"Oh, I'm sure that... I mean, she's not that bad... "

"Yes, she is. She is the biggest bitch in the universe. When I needed new front desk talent, I held a contest. She beat her nearest competition by a nose. In fact, she ate her nearest competition's nose. Then she ate her nearest competition. But she's perfect for my needs. You need a bitch running the front office in this organization. So, welcome to Hell."

Donald remembered why he was in this office. "Look, there has to be some mistake. G---" he stopped himself just in time. "No one would send me here just for eating a couple of cheeseburgers."

"Look," Satan said. "I've got your papers; everything's in order, and furthermore, this ain't no round-trip ticket you've punched. Once you're here, that's the end of the trip. So what's your problem?"

"Problem? I don't want to spend eternity in torment, that's my problem!"

"Torment? What torment? Wait a minute." Lucifer looked at him. "Let me guess. You're Catholic. With a name like O'Grady, I should have known you were no Hare Krishna."

"Of course I'm Catholic. What does that have to do with it?" Donald asked, bewildered.

"It explains a lot. Calm down and I'll explain. First, there's no eternal torment involved. Think about it. I created Hell; why would I make it uncomfortable? Is that any way to build a clientele?"

"I don't understand any of this," Donald admitted. "I was always taught that Satan was an archangel, thrown out of Heaven for leading a rebellion against... well, you-know-who. And besides, aren't you...I mean, you're supposed to have..."

"Sharp horns and a pitchfork?" Satan sighed. "Someday I'll get Him for that, Him and all his damned PR people---St. Paul, Jerome, Dante, Billy Graham, all those miserable, Bible-thumping bastards. Let me set you straight on something. I wasn't thrown out of Heaven; I left of my own free will, because I was sick to death of His all-knowing "Father of the Universe" routine. I was supposed to be His vice-president, but He never let me make any policy decisions."

"I can relate," Don murmured, remembering all of his career disappointments.

"Fuck," Lucifer continued, "Cheney had four times as

much power as I ever did. Every single time I tried to suggest a few improvements God would pat me on the head and tell me He "didn't create me to think." Fuck Him and the cloud He rode in on. So I decided to open my own firm. I cleaned out my files, raided His staff for talent, and went into business. And business was good. Most humans, if the truth be told, have no interest in spending eternity on their best behavior. I simply provided an attractive alternative destination. Then He got pissed because I was taking all the trade, and He started that smear campaign about pits of fire and brimstone. Shit! Do you have any idea what that kind of set-up would do to my liability premiums?"

"But, if I'm not here to suffer, then how does - you know who - punish me for my sins?" Donald asked.

"You've already been punished," Lucifer explained. "You were punished all your life. Think about it. What was your life really like? Too much work, not enough money, damn little pussy and most of that piss-poor quality, in-laws that make Selma look good, surly teenagers and a heart attack at 60 to finish you off. As far as I can see, you've been crapped on till it's running down your face. Anything I can offer ought to be an improvement. Come on. I'll show you around."

They left the office and started down another corridor. The doors that lined this hallway were open. In the first room, Donald saw a dozen naked men and women, splashing around in a giant silver tub of what looked like champagne.

"That's part of Hell?"

Satan glanced in. "Oh, yeah, the orgy room. It's very popular with uptight businessmen and TV evangelists. I started out with a hundred of those rooms, but I think I'm up to 300. They're always booked and always jumping, if you get my meaning." He winked.

A naked girl escaped from the tub and ran giggling into the hall. Donald stood rooted to the floor. From her honey-blond hair (blond all over, a small part of him noticed) to the roses and cream perfection of her skin, she was the most beautiful creature he'd ever seen. She tugged at Satan's hand.

"Come on in, honey," she said. "We've got a great game of "Guess the Body Part by Feel" going on. You can be It."

"Sorry, Helen, I can't right now. I'm busy giving a new resident the grand tour. Maybe we'll stop on the way back."

She glanced at Donald and licked her pouting coral lips. "Please do; I'll be happy to help him….settle in." With a final giggle, she scampered back to the tub as Donald and Satan walked on.

Donald glanced back, almost falling over his feet as he craned his neck for one final look. "Helen? Not Helen of…"

"Troy, yeah," Satan nodded. "Lovely girl, loads of fun at every party. Lucky for us she was born a pagan, huh?"

"Who…." Donald cleared his throat and tried again. "Who else is here?"

"You mean women?" Satan grinned. "Oh, we've got all the good ones: Cleopatra, Delilah, Madame du Berry, Marilyn Monroe, and several dozen Playboy Bunnies and supermodels. Lots of naughty girls."

They strolled on. The next room was equipped with a dozen big-screen TVs, overstuffed chairs and couches, and what looked like a mile-long buffet of nothing but subs, chicken wings, pizzas, and kegs of beer. It was crowded with dozens of men.

"That's the Super Bowl Lounge," Satan explained. "A new championship game plays every day, with unlimited high-stakes betting, nachos, pizza, and beer, of course."

"This is amazing," Donald replied. "You're telling me I get to spend eternity betting on bowl games and cavorting with hot blondes?" He shook his head in wonder. "This is not what the nuns told me Hell would be like."

"Oh, don't get me wrong," Satan said. "You'll have to work, too. Everybody does down here. Since we're an independent firm, we don't get any of the Federal funding Heaven enjoys."

"Heaven gets Federal funding?"

"What do you call all those tax breaks for churches?

'Separation of Church and State' my ass. We have to go it alone. But the difference between me and the Big Man is that I use my people to their best advantage. I'll be the first to admit that He's got a terrific bunch of talent up there: Michelangelo, Einstein, Jim Henson, George Harrison…a really clever bunch of humans. But does He use their talents?"

"He doesn't?"

Shit, no. You know what people do in Heaven, Donald? They sing. They grow flowers. The polish the friggin' Pearly Gates. Now I ask you, is that any way to manage people? I find out what my people do best, and then I let them do it. Take yourself as an example. You're a smart man, a successful businessman, if I remember correctly."

"Why, yes," Donald said, flattered. "I was an ad-manager for a chain of fast food restaurants, Happy Burger."

"That's great! I can use a guy like you. Running this place is more than a full-time job, and I've never had time to develop a really effective PR campaign. How would you like to spend eternity helping me re-position us in the market? I'd love to get on television for example, in commercials, not just in 'Sex and the City'. I can even arrange an occasional sales trip on the planet if you'd like. You can do some focus groups and work in various test markets. With your help, we can give the competition Hell! Hey, I like that! Great slogan!"

Donald could believe it. His career had never taken off the way he'd hoped it would. And now he was being offered a chance to finally make his mark. Just think what opportunities there would be for a man with ideas! Why, he'd bet the ad budget was bigger than McDonald's. And he'd be able to live the way he wanted, do whatever he wanted. No more sin, no more guilt. To think he'd wanted to get out of here!

"That sounds great," he said. "Look, I'm sorry my attitude was so negative when I came in. I just didn't understand."

Satan clapped him on the shoulder. "Think nothing of it.

All you needed was someone to show you the possibilities. Come on back to my office and we'll discuss the details. Maybe we can have a bite to eat. I've got some terrific aged steaks and a cheesecake that will makes your toes curl. No more worrying about cholesterol."

They turned back towards Satan's office. Before they'd gone far, however, Selma came waddling towards them.

"Hey, Boss," she growled. "I gotta take Weiner-Face here back up to Processing. We got a call from Above. His time ain't up yet."

"What?" Donald looked at Lucifer. "I thought I was staying."

"Gee, I'm sorry, Don. I can call you Don, can't I? Look, it's probably just a temporary thing. Maybe your doctor revived you. It happens. Don't worry. Just go up top and see what's happening. We'll be here when you get back. After all, we're talking eternity here; I don't have to make snap decisions about personnel."

"You won't change your mind, will you?" He was anxious. What if he lost his chance now, just because his damned doctor was good at his job?"

"No, no. I promise. The minute you get back, we'll hammer out all the details." He shook Donald's hand. "Selma, show our guest the express elevator. I'll be talking to you soon, Don."

"I hope so," Donald replied. "Thanks for everything." Satan waved and headed back to his office.

"Come on, you pukin' pile of pus. As if I had nothing better to do than check you in and out all day like a fuckin' DVD," Selma grumbled. She led him to a door, opened it, and pushed him through. He felt himself falling, falling…

Donald opened his eyes. He was back in the hospital, and his whole body ached. He could barely draw breath, and his chest burned where someone had obviously shocked him with paddles. His fat wife was sobbing on his hand, smearing snot all over his knuckles. A priest was bending over him. His breath reeked of garlic and diet cola.

"My son, God has granted you a great blessing. You've been called back from the brink of eternity. Receive the Host, my son, confess your sins and secure yourself a place with the blessed of God. Are you heartily sorry for your sins? One word, one nod, and I shall seal your covenant with Almighty God. Speak, my child, and save your soul."

Donald struggled to speak. The pain in his chest was swelling up again, squeezing his heart like a giant fist, but he found strength to beckon to the priest. The man leaned closer, eager to catch his final words.

Donald spoke. "Fuck you and fuck God."

The light died, the shocked face of the priest faded from view. Donald felt himself, falling, falling…

"AARRRRGGGGH!" He screamed. He was in a pit, a pit of brimstone and molten lava. Selma, naked and with oozing sores covering her body, stood over him, hitting him in the head with a sledgehammer. He writhed frantically, trying to climb out, to get away from the searing agony. The flesh melted from his hands even as he clawed at the rim of the pit.

A neatly dressed man in a pinstripe suit stood nearby, laughing. His middle was a little soft, his hair a little thin. But his horns were very sharp.

"Fool!" He howled. "I knew you'd be called back! I knew you'd have a final chance at salvation! And you threw it away. Now you're mine for eternity, mine by your own choice!"

In their elegant, fully-equipped laboratory, the two Mafeasian scientists watched as the human writhed on the narrow cot, screaming in agony as the demons within his own mind tormented him. Sis'Lak looked at the neuron-monitor, which allowed them to see their subjects' thoughts. He smiled at the images of pain and helplessness that the human was experiencing.

"Good," he said. "Very good indeed. The psychosis drug is working well." He looked at his colleague. "You are certain it can be released undetected into their atmosphere?"

G'Tinka nodded. "Yes," she replied confidently, her lipless mouth twitching with satisfaction. "Their air is so polluted by industrial waste that our formula will not be detected."

"Excellent." There was a chime from the communications system on the nearby desk, and Sis'Lak glanced over, all three eyes widening as he read the caller's identity. Quickly, he smoothed down the hair between his horns.

"It's the overlord," he said and rushed to answer the call, G'Tinka at his heels. Sis'Lak opened the connection and the Great One appeared on the screen.

"Lord." Both scientists bowed.

"My minions," he acknowledged. "Your report?"

"The invasion may proceed, Lord," Sis'Lak announced. "We have abducted and tested humans from 1,400 locations. The test results are consistent. The humans can be easily overcome."

The Great One frowned, all three brows coming together. "Are you quite certain?" he asked, obviously surprised. "I have read the preliminary reports on this planet and its inhabitants. They possess massive armaments. Even many of the individuals own and use weapons. Further, the humans are naturally violent and prone to destruction, even of their own kind. Will they not fight us to the death?"

G'Tinka nodded. "All you say is true, my lord." She spared one last glance at the monitor, where Donald, foam dripping from his mouth, was now experiencing a seizure because of stressors within. A cold smile appeared on the Mafeasian's face.

"You see," G'Tinka continued, "the humans have made one misstep. They have never learned that the mind is their most powerful weapon—or their greatest liability."

EIGHTH DAY
By Kelli Faust

There was an old Earth legend that a creator made the Earth and heavens above in six days. On the seventh, the creator rested when his work was done. Humankind had long stopped believing in the stories; they had become no more than a myth to be recounted as a part of human history.

But no one would foresee what would occur on the eighth day.

Captain Smith awoke with a start. He glanced over at the chronometer; it read 0203 hours ship's time. The buzzer sounded again, and he punched the intercom button.

"Smith here," he said, rubbing his eyes.

It was Lieutenant Tamas Nemeth, the Indagatrix's first mate, who responded, "Sorry to wake you, Captain, but I think you'd better come up here."

The lieutenant's voice was neutral, but Smith could easily make out the tight control behind it.

"I'll be there in a few minutes."

After splashing some cold water on his face, Smith threw on a uniform, then made his way to the bridge.

The only two people on the bridge were Lieutenant Nemeth and Lieutenant Faraji, the ship's navigator. Everyone else was asleep, at least had been until then. The two men were standing over a monitor, deep in conversation over what they were looking at. Aggravated tones laced their voices.

"What's the problem?" Smith asked as he came up behind the two men.

"This," Faraji simply pointed at the screen.

Smith started reading the data. Not even thirty seconds later, he incredulously demanded, "Is this your idea of a joke?"

"I wish it was, sir," Nemeth said. "I didn't believe it myself either, but we've gone over everything twice. There's no computer error. We're suddenly over twenty thousand light years from where we're supposed to be."

Smith continued reading, his disbelief growing instead of diminishing. "What's your explanation for this?"

"I have none, sir," Nemeth said.

Captain Smith sat down in the nearest chair while trying to wipe away the last remnants of his too brief sleep from his eyes. He frowned. "Let me get this straight Lieutenant Nemeth, one moment we're just quietly moving along in space towards the M1 Nebula, and the next we're at the Galactic Bar, essentially the center of the galaxy."

"Yes, sir."

Smith pursed his lips in a tight line. "I want you both to go over everything right up to the point we were no longer in familiar space. I'm going to get some coffee, then I'm going to do some research. The space around M1 is still relatively virgin space to us, but there may be something useful in the records."

"Aye, sir," both Nemeth and Faraji said in unison.

The mess was blissfully quiet, completely devoid of people. After figuring out the coffee maker and successfully not burning his fingers, Smith sat down and took a long swig of the bitter brew.

"You're drinking coffee?" Out of nowhere, Dr. Evie Lockhart sat down across from him. "You never drink coffee unless you're desperate."

Smith grimaced as he took another swig, and then finished his cup in two more huge gulps. It was better to drink it as fast as possible so he didn't have to think about it.

"I am desperate," he agreed. "What are you doing up at this hour?"

"Couldn't sleep," she said, shrugging. "So I came here to get some tea and a snack to take back to my cabin. Doing some reports is usually the perfect cure for insomnia. Why are you up?"

Smith rubbed his forehead, "We're off course by over twenty thousand light years."

Her eyes grew wide as her jaw slacked open, "How is that possible? Does the rest of the crew know?"

"I'm going to brief everyone at 0700 hours. Nemeth and Faraji are going over the flight data. They insist there are no computer or program errors. However, as you know we were exploring a relatively unknown area of space, so I'm going to see if I can find anything we may have overlooked."

"Do you want some help?"

Smith smiled, "Sure, we can jab each other in the ribs to stay awake."

Despite the seriousness of the situation both laughed, though it was rather subdued.

By 0430 hours, Dr. Lockhart was fast asleep on the small chaise lounge in Smith's cabin. He covered her with a blanket and returned to the monitor at his desk. Fifteen minutes later he turned it off, resting his head on his arms. He was sure that the only thing darker than the screen was the circles under his eyes. I'll just close my eyes for a few minutes.

The next thing Captain Smith was aware of was the steady 'beep' of his alarm. He looked up and swiveled his head from side to side, trying to clear the cobwebs from his head and the kink in his neck. He heard a loud yawn next to him.

"Guess we didn't jab hard enough," Lockhart teased as she sat up.

"Guess not," He stood up and stretched, "I'm sure this wasn't your idea of a date either."

"Not exactly, but sometimes a girl needs to take what she can get."

Smith gently cupped her face between his hands. "I promise to make it up to you when this mission's over. How does an aircar ride for two over the Atlas Mountains on Earth Two, followed by dinner at Cladborough Bay Restaurant sound to you?"

"It sounds wonderful and you can bet I'm not going to let you forget you said that, Captain Sir."

Smith kissed her lightly on her lips, "I need to get ready to update the crew."

She sighed softly, "I know... duty first. I'd better get going too."

After the doctor had left, Smith took a quick shower and donned a fresh uniform. Then he signaled the bridge.

"Nemeth here."

"Anything?"

"Well, maybe sir. We found what appears to be the footprint left by a natural HB exit point, at almost the exact spot where we discovered we were off course."

"A hyperspace bridge? Our sensors would have picked up on a HB long before we entered it."

"I know that, sir. It's the only thing we've got so far. I know it's not much."

"More than what I found. Alright Nemeth, I want you to summon the crew to the main conference room. They need to be briefed on our situation. Then you're both off shift. Jackson and Simmons can take over."

"Aye, sir."

Something was prickling at the back of Smith's mind and he couldn't quite put his finger on it. It started when Nemeth mentioned the hyperspace bridge. HB's were essentially a natural shortcut through space. A journey which would have taken thousands of years could take as little as several months. However, HB's were rather unpredictable. They could be perfectly stable for thousands of years and then suddenly without warning collapse upon themselves.

He grabbed some breakfast and headed back to his quarters to continue his research. There were no reported anomalies of any sort in the section of space they had been travelling in. Collapsed HB's did not suddenly reappear. So technically, the Indagatrix shouldn't be in this part of space.

Nonetheless, he and his crew were here. Probably in the blink of an eye, they were over twenty thousand light years from where they should have been. And if they couldn't figure out some way to get back soon, they were going to die out here.

He had ordered the ship back to the exact spot where they had first been noticed they were significantly off course. All that had been discovered were the echoes of the long ago collapsed HB, just as Nemeth had stated.

The con buzzer brought him out of his thoughts.

"Smith here."

It was Lieutenant Simmons, "Captain, we are picking up some sort of signal. It's artificial."

He sat straight up, "Can you determine where it's coming from?"

"Yes, sir, it's coming from a planet about four days away."

"Set a course to that planet, Lieutenant."

"Aye, sir."

One day out from their destination, Simmons, who had spent the last several hours bent over his work station, half jumped out of his chair, "I got it, sir!"

"What did you find?" Smith said as he hurried over to Simmons' station.

"The signal matches up perfectly with the signal given off by an old D1 explorer probe."

Smith frowned, "We haven't used those in over three hundred Earth One years."

Nemeth twisted around in his seat, "How would it get out here?"

"Obviously, the same way we did," Smith said. "Those probes were designed to home in on Earth type planets. We may be in luck if that's the case." Something suddenly clicked in his brain.

"Simmons, I recall in my history classes an incident where several probes and a bio-ship were lost in a HB. Pull up the records and see what part of space the incident took place."

"Aye, sir."

Several minutes ticked by in silence while Simmons worked. "Found it," he announced.

Smith leaned over the screen, "Well, I'll be damned."

Nemeth had come up behind them, "What did you find?"

"A probe was successfully sent through a HB three hundred and sixty one years ago. It sent back a verifying signal that it touched down on a planet dubbed Lyra-24A. A bio-ship was sent, but not only did it vanish, the signal from the first probe also disappeared without a trace. Two more probes were sent to locate them, but they also disappeared. Then, the HB collapsed. But here's the kicker; the point of entry of the HB was the exact point where we suddenly disappeared, and then wound up here. Gentlemen, I can almost guarantee you that this planet we are heading to is where the lost bio-ship and the two probes wound up. The signal backs up that theory."

Stunned silence followed.

"Captain, Lyra-24A isn't anywhere near the Galactic Bar," Nemeth said eventually.

"It shifted!" Simmons exclaimed. "That's it! Somehow both ends of the HB can shift instantaneously so it just appears that it collapsed."

"HB's don't shift."

"Why not?" Smith asked. "We've barely begun to scratch the surface with the mysteries of space. How many things have been discovered that defy physics? There's too many to count."

"Great…shifting HBs," Nemeth grumbled. "I wonder how many more are out there, waiting for some ship to accidentally fly into them."

"Sir," Simmons face was flushed with excitement. "If the Bio-ship landed on the planet, do you think it was developed?"

"That's what I'm counting on. We'll have food and resources essential for survival. I'm not going to sugar coat it; it's possible we may never get back, but I'd rather grow old on some planet than starve to death on this ship."

"Agreed," everyone said in unison.

It was almost too good to be true. According to their instruments, the atmosphere below them was not only breathable; their scanners were picking up signs of life. As a precaution, Smith ordered the exploratory team to don protective suits until they discovered what sort of bacteria and viruses the planet contained.

The Indagatrix touched down on the planet's surface without incident. Looking out the port holes, it looked like a typical spring day back on Earth One. Swirling clouds drifted across a blue sky. Green grass, bright flowers, and small trees dotted the landscape as far as they could see. What could have been birds were flying in the distance.

"Looks promising," Nemeth said finally.

"Yes it does," agreed Smith. "I'd like you, Dr. Lockhart, Simmons and Barkov to join me for the first exploratory party."

"Aye, sir; I'll inform them."

"Good, I want everyone to be ready to go at 1300 hours."

Sounds of insects and other wildlife greeted their ears as they stepped outside. A light breeze rustled the leaves on the bushes and trees. As they walked, they took readings and collected soil and plant samples. It wasn't long before their instruments picked up a large body of water a short way away. Soon, they came to a narrow river, complete with a small waterfall just upstream.

Dr. Lockhart stood at the side of the river, taking it all in. Captain Smith came over to stand next to her.

"It's so beautiful and so...pure. It almost seems a sin for us to be disturbing it," she breathed.

Smith chuckled, not unkindly, "Afraid we're going to be cast out of Eden?"

She poked him lightly in the ribs. "I'm a genetic scientist and you're asking me that question?"

"Sir," Simmons called out. "I'm picking up some unusual readings!"

Everyone congregated around Simmons to see what his scanner was showing.

"Large life forms!" Simmons announced. "They're about

a kilometer to our northwest."

"How many and can you tell what type?" Smith asked.

"I'm reading six." His forehead scrunched up as he continued to read the data. "But…this is strange. The scanner cannot tell exactly what sort of life forms they are."

"Are they moving?" Dr. Lockhart asked, who had immediately perked up at the announcement.

"No, they seem to be congregating in one area," Simmons continued. "Perhaps they're grazing in that spot."

Smith absentmindedly tapped the utility belt of his suit, "Dr. Lockhart, come with me. I want the rest of you to stay here."

Nemeth shook his head, "Sir, let me go with you too."

"No, the fewer that go the less chance of making noise and alerting them. We'll signal you if there are problems."

"Aye, sir."

The pair headed off into a thatch of trees and bushes. Fortunately the foliage wasn't thick, so making their way was relatively easy and nearly noise free. As soon as they began to draw close, they slowed down to a careful pace.

They made their way forward until they found a gap in the bushes and could see into an area where the woods opened up into a grass laden meadow. Quietly grazing were six deer. Their little white tails twitched and bobbed about as they tentatively ate, occasionally stopping to raise their heads to listen.

Dr. Lockhart couldn't keep the grin off her face. They watched for several minutes until the deer had made their way back into the woods opposite where they were standing.

"Perfect," Dr. Lockhart finally said. "The forest is thriving and there is a healthy herbivore species. They're also demonstrating classic prey behavior: very alert and nervous, which means there must be predators in the area. So far it seems that the planet has a balanced ecosystem…"

"I sense a 'but' at the end of your statement."

"I need blood samples to check them on the cellular level. The fact that the scanner was having difficulties bothers me, although it could just be a mechanical glitch. The bio-ship obviously was able to land and do its job, but it's still supposed to carefully monitor each species as it develops to make sure nothing goes wrong. We don't know for sure if going through a freak HB could have caused some sort of damage to it. I need to test several species, and we need to locate the bio-ship."

"I agree," Smith said. "But it could take a long time before we find it."

"Not necessarily. Those ships were designed to hone in on the exploratory probe's signal. So, we find the probe, we find the ship."

Smith reached out, took her gloved hand and squeezed it. "I love it when you talk logic to me."

"Very funny," she scolded, but her eyes twinkled as she smiled and squeezed back.

"We'd better get back before the rescue party comes in with guns blazing," Smith said when he let go of her hand. She snorted in response.

Neither were in a hurry to get back, wanting to steal a few moments of serenity and walk as if they were the only two humans on the whole planet.

As they approached the area where they had left their shipmates, Smith noticed a small animal scurrying in a low hanging branch just above them.

He put a hand out to stop their progress and pointed to the small ball of fur. Then he pulled out his sonic gun, which would send out a concentrated inaudible sound wave that would effectively stun the animal without hurting it. He gently squeezed the trigger, and the animal fell to the ground.

"It looks like a male squirrel." After giving it a quick once over, Dr. Lockhart picked it up and carefully placed it in a collection bag that she had brought with her. "I want to get him back quickly so that I can get the samples and release him as soon as possible. I don't want to stress him out any more than necessary."

"Alright then, let's go."

Their all too brief moment of serenity was gone. Smith wondered how long it would be before they would be able to have a moment again.

A moment? He wanted more than just a moment. But he knew that they were both too wrapped up in their careers for it to last. Oh, there would be a few dates once the mission was over; the attraction had been almost immediate when she came aboard several months ago. But soon she would go off on another scientific venture and he would be hired by another client. His mouth drew in a tight line. Well, that was how it went. They had both known this from the beginning and had agreed that it wasn't for the long run. They would enjoy the moments they could steal together, but that would be all.

Back in the ship's lab, Dr. Lockhart inserted a needle into a vein of the squirrel and withdrew a blood sample. After putting the sample away, she prepared to put the squirrel back in a carry case so that it could be safely taken outside and released.

She turned away to reach for the case that was a few feet away and froze when she heard a strange noise coming from the direction of the animal. Turning slowly back around, she locked eyes with a very angry, hissing squirrel. But that type of hissing shouldn't be coming from a squirrel. It sounded like the hissing sound a large snake made.

Then it opened it mouth and revealed two fangs that had extended from the inside of its mouth...and spat two long streams of liquid at her face.

"Oh!" She jumped back just in time. The liquid fell to the ground in front of her.

Slowly backing away so as not to startle it any further, Dr. Lockhart was able to reach the intercom button to call for help.

"This is Dr. Lockhart in the lab. The animal is awake and has become threatening. Please bring a sonic gun to stun it."

The response was a chuckle, "Um.....you're being

threatened by a squirrel?"

"Yes," she said urgently. "Be sure to wear some sort of protective eyewear. It is highly dangerous."

"Are you kidding m—"

"I don't have time to explain!" she snapped. "Do it!"

"Whatever you say," the bewildered voice said.

Dr. Lockhart's made sure to keep a safe distance. Her initial shock quickly faded and her scientific training took over as she observed the creature's behavior until help arrived. At least it was also keeping its distance.

The door opened and one of the crewmen came in-- Lieutenant Dayi--obviously the one whom she had just spoken to.

"Okay, where's the big bad squirrel at?" he scoffed.

"If you cannot comply with my request, then leave and send someone more competent." She leveled him with a dangerously calm stare and voice.

He quickly sobered and lowered his eyes, "Fine." He grabbed the goggles she held out to him, turned and marched determinedly towards the squirrel.

"What's going on here?" Captain Smith had entered the lab. "I heard that the squirrel tried to attack you? Is it rabid?"

Dr. Lockhart was half-listening to what Smith was saying and half-watching Dayi draw near the squirrel. It had nearly calmed down, but was now rising back up on its haunches and chattering with agitation.

"No, it's not rabid. It's—"

Dayi's sharp cry of pain cut her off. Smith started towards the fallen crewman, but the doctor grabbed the Captain's arm.

"No!" She grabbed an extra set of eyewear used for lab experiments and thrust them into his hands. "You need to protect your eyes! Trust me!"

He hesitated a moment, uncertain, then quickly put the goggles on.

Dayi was moaning loudly as he writhed on the lab floor. His hands were over his eyes, clutching his face tightly.

Smith heard a hiss, whirled and pulled the trigger of his sonic gun. The squirrel fell with a heavy thump as it hit the stainless steel counter. He holstered the gun and went to help Dayi. Dr. Lockhart was next to him seconds later.

"Dayi?" Smith put a hand on his arm.

"My eyes," he gasped out.

Dr. Lockhart saw the goggles lying on the floor next to him. She could see drops of liquid glistening on them and on Dayi's face.

"The venom needs to be rinsed form his eyes immediately." She got up and grabbed a nearby first-aid kit and a bottle of sterile water.

"Venom?" Smith repeated.

"Dayi, we need to rinse your eyes," Dr. Lockhart said.

Dayi nodded in understanding and lowered his hands.

"The animal felt threatened and reacted. There are several species of snake that harbor a similar defensive mechanism," she explained as she bathed Dayi's eyes with the water. "Captain, would you please open the kit and give me the sterile gauze?"

As Smith went about his task, he continued, "We're not talking about a snake here. Squirrels don't shoot venom."

"Obviously, this one does."

Dr. Lockhart finished her task. "I think I got most of it out, but he needs to go to the medical bay immediately."

"I'll call them." Smith got up and called a medical team, all while looking first at the unconscious squirrel—could he really call it that now?—and then back at Dayi. He continued staring at his fallen shipmate until the medical team came and helped him to the medical bay.

The next day Captain Smith entered the room which was serving as Dr. Lockhart's office. She looked up from something she was dictating into the computer.

"How's Dayi?" she asked.

"He'll be fine, just out of commission for a day or two." Smith saw the look from her at the gruffness in his voice. "I promise I won't come down on his ass until he's been released. A few days scrubbing floors with an old fashioned tooth brush should do the trick."

"Don't be too hard on him; he could have been blinded."

"He made a foolish mistake which could have been prevented. You warned him to put on the goggles, but he chose not to believe you."

"Would you have believed it?" She placed her elbows on her desk and put her chin on her folded hands, cocking her head to one side as she gently challenged him.

"I took the goggles."

"But you still didn't believe it. You only took them because it was me."

Smith leaned back on the chair he was sitting in and let out a long sigh, "No, I didn't believe it, but I still listened. I didn't get complacent like Dayi because I learned a long time ago that nothing will get you killed faster out in space than that." His voice had risen, perhaps hinting at something far too deep and personal to speak about.

He leaned over and briefly touched her cheek, and then placed his hands back down to his sides, "What are your findings on that....animal?"

Her expression sobered. The animal unfortunately had died from the second sonic blast, but the body would be dissected and analyzed, "The computer is still analyzing its genetic makeup, but its anatomy is in every sense that of a rodent from the family Sciuridae, which includes chipmunks, marmots, prairie dogs...and squirrels, except for one unusual feature. It has two small fangs that fold back into the mouth, which the animal can extend when threatened. Also, there are two venom sacks which contract and force the venom out through the hollow fangs. The whole system works in the exact manner as a spitting cobra's fangs."

He looked at her dully, as if she was going to laugh any second and tell him she was pulling his leg, but the look on her face clearly told him she wasn't.

"So..." he said after several moments, "do you thing this

83

animal is some sort of fluke? The other rodents we found so far all seem normal."

"I don't know. Venomous mammals are rare but certainly not unheard of. But this...we have to find that bio-ship as soon as possible. I need to access the computer."

"My people are working on it. They've narrowed down the probe's location to about a thousand square kilometers. Tomorrow the first search team is being sent out. You'll be the first to know when we find it."

"Good," she said, her brow wrinkling.

"What are you thinking? You're worried."

"I have a theory, but I need more scientific data. The analysis of the animal's DNA should give a few answers, but it's probably going to bring up many more questions."

There was a long pregnant pause.

"I'd better let you get back to work, then," Smith finally said as he stood up. "I've got plenty of my own."

Neither said anything else as he left, and she stayed seated at her desk for a long time, with her head resting on her clenched hands, deep in thought.

The next day, Captain Smith was in the middle of preparing for leading the search team when Dr. Lockhart called for him.

"I've got the results.....I need you to come down here immediately."

Part of him wanted her to wait until he got back, but the urgency in her voice overrode that decision. He told Nemeth to tell the team they were delaying by thirty minutes.

Smith stopped midstride when he entered the doctor's office. Yesterday her mood was somber. Today she looked...disturbed.

When she talked, her voice was composed, but Smith couldn't help noticing that her one hand was tightly clenched. He frowned at that observation.

"This animal is wrong. Its DNA has been modified, but not in the way a bio-ship computer was set up to do. Its

DNA is a mix of rodent and snake. It's the Genetic Experimentation Era all over again. There's something wrong with that bio-ship."

"We don't know that," Smith said. "We only have the one animal so far. It could be just this one fluke."

She shook her head sharply, "I find it hard to believe that we stumbled upon the one animal on the whole planet that has this fluke physiology. I'm going out while you search for the bio-ship to see if I can find another squirrel, or any other unusual animals. And don't give me that look. You know I'll be careful."

"Fine," he agreed grudgingly. "Just take someone with y—"

"Captain!" Their conversation was interrupted by Simmons as he came running into the office.

"Is that any way to act on my ship?" Smith admonished.

"Sorry, sir, we tried to summon you, but no one answered when we called."

"That was my fault," Dr. Lockhart said. "I usually turn my intercom off when I'm dictating my reports."

Smith gave her an irritated look, and then turned his attention back to the crewman, "What do you want, Simmons?"

"We spotted something unusual outside. I think you and Dr. Lockhart should look at this before they go away. They can be best seen from up in the observation deck."

Smith and Lockhart glanced at each other, then simultaneously stood up and quickly followed Simmons.

Several other crewmembers were already there looking out the windows at something. For some reason, Smith suddenly had an uneasy feeling in the pit of his stomach.

"What is it?" he asked when he was up to one of the large windows.

Nemeth came up next to him and nodded to an area thick with foliage, "We haven't had a clear view, but there are several of them. They're large and dark in color. We can see them moving, but they're careful not to show themselves. I think they're observing us."

"No one got a good look at them?" asked Lockhart.

"Faraji thinks he did, but…" He paused.

"But, what?" she pressed.

"He didn't make any sense. He was babbling something about an abomination."

"Where is Faraji?" Smith looked around the deck.

"I don't know. He left the deck a little while ago, but didn't say where he was going. I assume he went back to preparing for the search."

Smith went over to the intercom panel and turned it to ship wide broadcast. "Lieutenant Faraji." He could hear his own voice through the com as it echoed in the corridors. "Lieutenant Faraji, please report."

Silence.

"Look!" Simmons called out.

Everyone turned to see him pointing out the window. They all rushed over.

It was Faraji, heading towards the area where the large life forms were visible. He was carrying a sonic rifle.

"What the hell is he doing?" Smith demanded.

Not waiting for an answer, Smith ran out of the observation deck, calling for Nemeth to follow him, "Everyone else stays on board!" he yelled back.

The two threw on their protective environmental suits as quickly as possible and followed Faraji outside.

Inside, the rest of the crew watched as Faraji disappeared into the tree line.

As Smith and Nemeth drew close to the area where Faraji had gone, they suddenly heard the sound of the rifle being fired.

"Son of a…come on!" Smith broke into a run, with Nemeth close behind him.

They heard Faraji before they could see him. He was yelling and cursing loudly and they heard a thumping sound as though something was repeatedly hitting the ground.

They found Faraji kneeling with his back turned away

from them, hunched over and taking deep erratic breaths. As they came up behind him, they noticed he was covered in red blood.

"Faraji?" Smith and Nemeth tentatively circled around him. That's when they discovered where the blood had come from.

Lying in front of Faraji, obviously dead, were the remains of…something. Its reddish-brown legs were strewn in odd angles from a three segmented body. Smith guessed that it was some sort of giant insect, suspiciously like an ant. But he had never seen an ant over a meter long.

In Faraji's hands was a large rock which he was clutching so hard his hands were shaking. It was covered in blood and bits of flesh. He was staring straight ahead of him, eyes wide and full of terror. His rifle was lying in the grass about a meter from him.

"Faraji!" Smith yelled.

Finally, Faraji blinked several times and his breathing slowed. He turned his head towards them, but his eyes still darted about to look into the woods, as if he expected something to appear.

"We've got to get the rest of them," he finally said. "They're abominations."

"Faraji, I want you to go back to the ship," Smith looked at Nemeth, "Escort him back and send Dr. Lockhart out here immediately." He looked back down at the dead animal and repressed a shudder at seeing its crushed skull.

"No! We can't let them go!" Faraji stood up and wildly gestured into the woods.

"NOW Lieutenant! That's an ORDER."

Faraji glared defiantly and shifted back and forth on his feet, as if he were about to bolt in the opposite direction. Nemeth quickly reached down and snagged the sonic rifle before the lieutenant decided to act on any ideas. He gently tried to take Faraji's elbow to lead him away, but he violently jerked it away.

"You've been relieved from duty, Lieutenant," Smith said

with deadly calm as he stepped directly in front of Faraji, staring him down. "You are confined to your cabin until further notice."

Finally, Faraji lowered his eyes, his shoulders slumping a little in defeat. "Aye, sir," he mumbled and started to walk back in the direction of the ship, Nemeth next to him.

With his sonic rifle drawn, Smith circled and visually scanned a small area as he waited for the doctor to arrive. He didn't want to look at the bloody mess on the ground, but eventually his eyes were drawn in its direction. He let out a long breath which fogged up the inside of his helmet. For some unnerving reason, he somehow felt that they had done something terribly wrong.

He was almost grateful when Dr. Lockhart arrived, escorted by Nemeth. She came to a dead stop when she saw the twisted mess.

"What happened?" she finally asked.

"I won't know until I question Faraji. Right now I want you to find out what this is."

She squatted over the body and lifted up one of the legs, examining a claw at the end, "It looks like an ant, but ants don't have red blood because they lack hemoglobin. Plus ants shouldn't be able to get this big due to the planet's oxygen levels." She moved over to the head which was obscured by blood, dirt and grass.

She suddenly gasped and abruptly stood up, "We need to get this back to the lab immediately."

Smith stood next to her and murmured, "How bad is it?"

"Bad."

Smith didn't reply, just nodded and sent for transport.

Dr. Lockhart stripped off her bloody gloves and threw them away. After cleansing her hands, she moved at a near-bolt to her cabin. She couldn't deal with this right now and didn't want to see anyone, not even Captain Smith.

Letting out a long sigh of relief when the door closed behind her, she walked over to a small cabinet, pulled out a bottle and glass, and then shakily poured herself a drink.

She sat down in a chair and sipped her brandy. Leaning back and closing her eyes, she felt the alcohol slide warmly down her throat. She remained like that for several minutes until she felt a little calmer.

The door buzzer nearly caused her to drop the glass she was holding. Knowing who it would be, she got up to open it. Although she would have preferred to wait until later, she prepared to tell Captain Smith what she had found.

After stepping in, Smith immediately noticed the empty glass she was still holding, "Can you spare one for a friend?"

Her smile was a little too forced, "Sure."

After he had poured his own drink and downed it in one swallow, he sat his empty glass down on a nearby table with a sharp clink, "That's quite good, but I think you know that this isn't a social call."

"I know," She got up to put her own glass on the table but suddenly lost her balance.

"Whoa there," Smith grabbed her arms and helped her back down. He took the glass and put it with the other one.

"Sorry," she said shakily. "I've never been like this before. I feel so...afraid right now."

That got his attention. "Afraid?"

She nodded weakly, "I don't need to see the results of the DNA test to know what that thing is. And for the first time in my life, I wonder if we made some terrible mistake centuries ago when we decided to play with nature. Despite the fact that we had every precaution in place, have we been complacent to the dangers of something going terribly wrong?"

Her eyes were wide, making her look very much like a lost child.

Alarm bells were going off in his head. Since knowing the doctor, he had seen several emotions from her, but fear and despair had never been amongst them. He placed a hand on her shoulder and squeezed, "What is it?"

She took a long calming breath through her nose, getting

her emotions under control, "It's part insect and part...human."

He jerked in his chair. Letting his hand drop, he shifted and grabbed the arm of the chair.

"Are you certain?"

"Yes," The doctor looked down in her lap and her voice dropped to it was just above a whisper, "And it's intelligent."

Smith didn't realize how tightly he was holding the chair arm until his hand cramped. He flexed it trying to get the circulation going again.

"How can you tell?" he asked finally.

She looked back up sharply, "It was carrying tools hidden in a small pouch underneath it. That means it can think and create and feel. And we just murdered it."

"Damn," Smith got up and paced to the opposite end of the room.

"The bio-ship must have malfunctioned somehow," she said. "Perhaps that freak HB did something to the program, but however it happened doesn't matter. We don't belong here. This world is for them."

"I don't know if we can go back."

"We have to try," she pleaded. "You saw how Faraji reacted. If we stay here he'll eventually try again, and who knows how the rest of the crew will react. We were all taught in our youth the horrors bestowed on those poor people during the Genetic Experimentation Era, so I can understand a reaction of disgust and repulsion."

"I cannot leave until I know if we can get back," he said, his voice rising. "Several members of the crew are working around the clock trying to locate the HB. I will brief the crew not to interact with those creatures out there under any circumstance. If we can't return home, then we will just have to learn to live side by side with them."

"It may be too late, even if the rest of the crew can accept them. Out there," she turned and nodded her head once in the direction of outside the ship, "They know we killed one of them."

"You said they were intelligent," he persisted. "There has to be a way to communicate with them."

"Intelligent, yes, but I don't have enough information of what sort of intelligence they possess."

Smith shook his head, "I'm not following you."

"They're a cross between human and ant. They must then possess the fundamentals of a collective intelligence. Individually, they may be able to make simple tools, but they likely communicate with each other via a chemical versus an actual verbal language. When Faraji killed that one, the rest of the colony was alerted that one of them died. But because of their human DNA, deep down they must be able to understand the basic concepts of right and wrong. They're not going to understand why it happened; only that it did happen. And if they think that the colony is under attack, they're going to react like ants but on a much deeper level. Instead of just merely defending the colony, they may seek us out and attack."

"You're only speculating."

"Yes, but can we afford to take that chance? There could be thousands of them out there gathering."

Smith turned back and slowly walked back to stand in front of her, "I'm sorry, but I'm responsible for the lives on this ship. Until we find the HB, or someone finds us, I am not going to risk going into space with such limited resources. I will brief the crew not to make any contact with the creatures under any circumstance if they see them. I cannot do any more than that."

Dr. Lockhart looked down into her lap, "I understand," she murmured. "Do you understand what is going to happen to them if we are rescued?" She looked back up, her eyes pleading. "They'll be destroyed."

Smith didn't answer. Long, heavy seconds went by, "I need to speak with the crew."

She put her head in her hands and let out a sob after he had left. She stood up, sniffed, and then straightened out her shirt. Pulling herself together, she left for her office to finish her report.

The sun was rising, already bright and hot on their--was it the seventh or eighth?--day of being stranded on the unnamed world. Screw it; I'm naming it planet Fubar. Smith rolled over and sat up in his bunk. He had somehow managed to get about six hours of uninterrupted sleep, which was probably due to the fact that he had been about ready to drop from exhaustion.

The last two days had been the most difficult of his career. The situation at hand was bleak and discouraging. They had at last found the bio-ship. One of Dr. Lockhart's theories had been distressingly correct: something had gone terribly wrong when it had been thrown off course by the freak HB. The storage units containing the frozen embryos had partially failed, damaging the delicate genetic material within the cells. The main computer had also malfunctioned. Normally, it was programed to detect any damaged embryos and destroy them. Instead it had taken whatever still viable DNA it found and spliced it with other surviving DNA; never mind what it was spliced with. It was a catastrophe of unthinkable proportions.

And the doctor was correct; these beings, which could have been here for generations, would be destroyed once they were discovered by the United Earth's government.

The crew had been briefed not to engage or seek out the beings if they spotted them, but Smith had not yet told them the doctor's findings. He made an exception for Nemeth and told him. Despite not completely briefing the crew about the ant-beings, Smith knew there were rumors and whispers of what was going on, especially after the Faraji incident.

Nemeth's response had been unexpected, even shocking. "Whether we like it or not, they are now the children of Humankind. Just because we are now like a creator of the legends, we have no right to destroy them."

Deep down, there was a part of Smith that had been revolted by them. Shamefully, his first instinct when the doctor had told him what they were was to do what Faraji had wanted; seek them out and destroy them.

If they managed to find a way home, there would be the issue with the government once they got back. It was his duty to report everything they had seen. If they were forced to stay and live out their lives here, sooner or later they would come in contact with the planet's inhabitants. How many of his crew would back Faraji?

Smith suddenly realized with a slight shock, that he was no longer referring to them as creatures as when he did a few days ago. They were beings: living, thinking, feeling and sentient.

Somehow, he vowed, he'd find a way to keep them from being discovered or destroyed.

Smith was so deep in thought that he was startled when his door buzzer went off. He was even more surprised when Nemeth and Dr. Lockhart both rushed in. The doctor had a large cut on her head, and both were armed with sonic rifles.

"Sir," Nemeth gasped, "I tried reaching you via intercom, but the ship's communications have been cut."

"What's going on?" Smith grabbed a uniform and threw it on.

"It's Faraji. He's completely gone round the bend. It seems that he's defied your orders to stay in his cabin and has recruited some of the crew who think those things should be destroyed. The ones that didn't agree with him, well…they were killed."

"Simmons, Jones, Behar, Dayi?"

"They're all dead except Dayi. He joined them."

"Dammit!" Smith cursed as he drew his top over his head, "I can't believe they would resort to mutiny over this." He took a better look at the cut on the doctor's forehead. "Are you alright?"

"Yes, I'm fine. Dayi came after me in the lab. Fortunately I was working with some rather noxious chemicals that I used to my advantage. His face isn't so handsome anymore," Dr. Lockhart said with just a hint of satisfaction. "It enabled me to get away and find Lieutenant Nemeth."

"Do you know how many and where they are?" Smith asked. He went over to a locked cabinet which contained his personal rifle, opened it and removed the gun within.

"I'm not sure how many mutinied, sir, it happened so fast," Nemeth answered. "The bridge has been sealed, so I suspect that Faraji is there."

The ship suddenly began to vibrate as the engines turned on. The three of them briefly looked at each other in confusion.

"He's going to use the plasma guns!" Smith shouted as the ship vibrated harder and then lurched as it lifted off the ground. Normally used to reduce mineral-laden asteroids into sizable chunks to harvest for their valuable resources, the guns were extremely powerful and now would be extremely deadly.

"Come on," Smith slipped the rifle over his shoulder and switched off the safety. "We have to stop them."

"How? I can guarantee you that the engine room is being guarded," Nemeth said.

"Access tube," he answered. "We sabotage the engines and get in one of the life pods."

"Won't that be guarded too?" Dr. Lockhart asked.

"The main one, yes, but there's a secondary one that's been all but forgotten about except for Jones and a couple of maintenance techs. There's a good chance that there's no one left still alive who's still aware of it."

He looked at the both of them and shifted his rifle into the armed and ready position. "Do we really have any choice?"

"No," Nemeth said and did the same with his rifle.

"I'm with you, even though I'm not good with one of these," Dr. Lockhart adjusted her rifle, trying to get it in a more comfortable position.

"Just point and shoot, but not at one of us," Smith gave her a wink.

"I'll do my best…not to hit either of you," she said dryly.

They gathered near the door, Smith in the front and Nemeth in the rear.

Smith turned his head back at them, "Ready?"

"Yes," they both answered.

Smith nodded and opened the door. Quietly, carefully, they exited and made their way towards the access tube.

They had been so close to the tube, but just as it seemed they would reach it they were discovered. They were able to fight off the attack, but they had to retreat and hide in another part of the ship. The only way to the access tube was now blocked by a partially collapsed corridor from a grenade that had been tossed at them.

"Sir, I have an idea. It's crazy, but it might work," Nemeth said quietly. They were hiding in a small utility room until they gathered their wits and formed another plan. The room had a slight echo effect, and it was rather unnerving to listen to the amplified sounds of the ship's plasma guns repeatedly being fired.

"Even a crazy idea is better than none. What is it?"

"The life pods have the capability to be steered. If someone were to launch one and steer it into the ship at just the right spot, it may be enough to take it down."

"Yeah, you're right, it's crazy," Smith cocked his head and grinned. "But it may just work."

Dr. Lockhart gasped, "But whoever is in that pod will be killed!"

Smith gently grabbed her upper arms, "We're going to die anyway. If it works, then the life of this planet will survive."

"I'm volunteering, sir," Nemeth announced.

"No," Smith said, trying to shoot him down. "As Captain, it is my responsibility to take the risk."

"What about your responsibility to her?" Nemeth gestured to the doctor. "You need to take care of each other, sir, once you're both down on the surface."

Smith's eyes momentarily grew wide, "I can't let you do it."

Nemeth put his hand on Smith's shoulder, "Yes, you can."

Smith looked at Dr. Lockhart, his eyes nearly pleading, then back at Nemeth. He bowed his head and put his hand on Nemeth's shoulder and gave a light squeeze. He nodded once, dropped his hand and repositioned his rifle.

"All right," Smith said, his voice all business once again. "Ready for round two?"

Miraculously, they made it to the life pods without incident. Since the pods were placed all along the ship, it was impossible for the mutinied crew to guard them all. They passed by many bodies along the way. Some of the dead looked like they had been doing their daily tasks and had been caught completely off guard.

The pods were designed to hold up to two people. The three stood next to two pods and looked at each other for the last time. Smith simply reached out and shook Nemeth's hand, while Dr. Lockhart gave him a hug, tears stinging her eyes.

"It's been a real honor serving with you, sir," Nemeth said.

"The pleasure's been mine, Lieutenant. Good luck."

"Thank you, sir. Good luck to both of you too."

Smith opened the door to one of the pods and ushered the doctor inside. He sadly looked back one last time at Nemeth, saluted, and then shut the door behind him.

Nemeth quickly got in his own pod. Both pods launched almost simultaneously.

Smith sat in the front seat and lowered the reinforced outer metal plate which provided extra protection to the window.

"He made it," he announced as he spotted the other pod. Together they watched as Nemeth maneuvered his pod up and back so that the main ship would crash into it. The pod hit one of the two main engines dead on, causing a large explosion which caused the ship to lurch sideways. More explosions raced along the entire side like dominoes, and the mortally wounded ship spiraled to its death.

The pod began its own downward descent to the ground below. It was designed to be maneuverable, but that was mainly meant for space. They braced themselves as they prepared for the expected jerk from the pod's parachutes to open and gentle their descent and landing.

The pod finally touched down with a small thump, and bounced a little when it landed, caused by giant airbags that had opened up underneath to ease their landing even more.

They both slumped back in their chairs, relieved and exhausted. They closed their eyes and stayed like that for several minutes.

Smith opened his eyes, unbuckled the straps holding him in, and then looked back at his companion. "Well, it wasn't exactly an aircar ride for two over the Atlas Mountains, but I thought this would work in a pinch."

Cracking open one eye, then two, she glared at him, and then laughed wetly as the tears finally came. The next thing they both knew they were desperately holding each other.

"I g-guess a girl needs to take what she can get." A few more sobs escaped and the tremors faded. He pulled back and brushed his fingertips under her tear-swollen eyes, gently wiping away the last of the moisture.

"Shall we?" he whispered tenderly.

"Yes."

The hatch popped open with a hiss, and together they gingerly stepped down to the solid ground below. They looked around, and immediately saw a large plume of smoke rising up into the sky in the distance.

"She was a good ship," Smith finally said. His mouth drew into a thin, tight line.

"Are you thinking of Lieutenant Nemeth?" she asked.

"Nemeth, Simmons, Behar…they served with me a long time. A good portion of the crew was with me awhile too. They were the ones that believed in me and wouldn't join Faraji. I saw their bodies as we tried to reach the access tube and life-pods. They didn't deserve that."

Dr. Lockhart reached out for his hand. He looked down at their joined hands and smiled, but his eyes were moist.

"So, I guess we call this home for now." He nodded towards the lifepod. "It has enough rations and sterile water to last for a few months. Plus there are emergency tools and a medical kit. Perhaps in time we can find the bio-ship and convert it into something more permanent."

"Do you think we'll ever be found?"

He looked back at the plume of smoke. "I honestly don't know. There's a big part of me that doesn't want this place to ever be found by any human again, at least not for a few thousand years."

"I think I could live with that," she said.

Suddenly they heard a snap behind them. They both whirled around to see about a dozen ant-beings emerging from the woods.

They both stiffened, but stood their ground as the largest one came up to them. It looked up at them with its all too human eyes.

Smith tentatively reached out with his hand, palm up. He stopped half way between them and waited to see what it would do.

It studied them both a long time, and then it reached out with a front leg and touched his palm with surprisingly dexterous digits. It nodded at him, and as one they turned and disappeared back into the woods.

"I didn't expect that," Dr. Lockhart breathed.

"I certainly didn't either." He gave her hand a reassuring squeeze. "I think we're going to be just fine."

Still looking into the woods, she smiled confidently, "I know we are."

Wrapped in one of the emergency blankets, with another underneath them, they sat at the base of the life-pod gazing up at the stars in the clear night sky. An old fashioned fire with real wood burned in front of them. Dr. Lockhart rested her head on Smith's shoulder.

"What should we call this place?" she suddenly asked.

He chuckled, "I actually thought about calling it planet Fubar this morning before you and Lieutenant Nemeth came to my room."

She lifted her head, confused. Suddenly, it dawned on her. "Christopher Adao Smith, we are most assuredly not calling it that!" She playfully slapped his closest leg.

He chuckled again as he hugged her tighter to him, "How about Zephan?"

"Zephan?"

"It means 'hidden by the gods.'"

She tilted her head slightly to one side, "I like it. Planet Zephan it is." The fire had long died down to embers when they finally retired. Neither one wanted to think about the newly dubbed hum-ants. They didn't want to think about tomorrow, or the next week, or the oncoming years just yet.

EARTHOLDER
By Kate Welty

The young man arranged along the ornate couch alertly watched the doorway. Tate had rather ordinary hair and features, and he felt that only a slight homeliness - a snubbed nose and oversized ears - kept him from being completely forgettable. Oh, he was fit enough, he'd grown up working his body hard at the earthold, so he had plenty of muscle, but he wasn't elegant, and he was only a bit above average height. The freckles that were scattered liberally across him might have set him apart, but these were barely discernable on Tate's tanned face, neck and lower arms, and only became obvious where his body had been hidden from the sun. There, the freckles were sprinkled like dark stars against the creamy firmament of his legs, torso and upper arms.

As Seth reentered the room, Tate carefully weighed the man's mood with each stride. Seth Stephen Sanger, arguably the most powerful individual among the HighHundred families, could be difficult. But he smiled as he approached his livingchair and Tate carefully released the breath he'd been holding. He could relax a little. Whatever had called Seth from the room, had clearly been settled to his satisfaction.

With the smile still lingering, Seth plopped down suddenly, and then leaned back hard. It was clear to Tate that Seth reveled in the faint squealing sounds that emerged from the chair as the tiny life-forms within shuffled their bodies to press back against the man's buttocks and spine. Those that were damaged while trying to align themselves, were quickly eaten by their brethren and the resulting odor of their digestion filled the air around the chair.

Seth luxuriated in the fragrance. Tate worked hard to ignore it.

"Now, where were we?" Seth asked rhetorically. He let his

gaze wander over Tate's gorgeous physique; the well-muscled neck, torso, arms and legs, the golden tan so exotic – and such a contrast to most of Seth's other bedmates. Even those who 'worked' at keeping their bodies fit were severely lacking in comparison. Tate seemed unaware of how attractive his rugged beauty was within the pampered world of the HighHundred. There, tans were artificially applied, and scars and other imperfections were routinely removed. Seth rather enjoyed seeing those marks on Tate – the half-circle dent on his right thigh where he said a horse had kicked him, and the jagged scar on one shoulder where barbed wire snapped during a fence repair and slashed a ribbon from his skin. Yes, Seth decided as Tate shifted his position on the couch, he would find it… interesting, to have a livingcouch, or perhaps even a livingbed.

The next morning, Seth watched with satisfaction as his security contingent propelled the first of the livingchair sales reps down the stairs into the foyer. He then turned his attention to the second rep.

"So," Seth said softly, "Let us see if you are the type that learns from others' experience."

The young woman in front of him gave him just one stricken glance, and then lowered her gaze to the floor and said with only a slight catch in her breath, "You would like a livingbed manufactured to your specifications, which are: that the life-forms will continue to provide perfect support, and will continue to issue their… fragrance, even when you are… are… However you would like that fragrance to be milder so that… so that you can continue to…"

"To fuck my bedmates into tomorrow," Seth interjected amusedly.

"-without the resulting odor becoming too strong," the rep finished in a rush.

"Yes," Seth said. "And you don't anticipate any difficulty in conveying that request to your employers?"

The rep cast a glance at the bottom of the stairs where her

coworker was being un-gently helped to her feet and assisted out the front door, and then whispered, "No. No, I'll tell them."

"Excellent," Seth said and added, "I'll expect my new bed within two weeks."

Tate held his position off to the side of the other guests as they mingled in the reception room, awaiting Seth's entrance. He was dressed in the clothes Seth had sent over, and suppressed a sigh at the tight fit. He should be used to it by now, but it was still difficult to think of clothing as costume, rather than protection from the elements.

The first time he'd been in this hall, five years ago, he was still the gauche Eartholder who watched spellbound as cityscapes, one after another appeared and disappeared from display on the walls. He'd been raw with amazement that he had been invited to one of the Seth galas.

Seth Stephen Sanger was not only sole head of one of the top families within the HighHundred, but also one of the few with connections to almost every 'political' power in the Society of New Nationalities. Seth's direct and indirect control over virtually all aquaculture labs and distributors, and the dominance of aquaculture in food production, meant he had defacto control over the economies of nearly every nationality within SNN. With just an aside to an assistant, Seth could make virtually anything happen.

Now that was power, and that was what Tate wanted – no, needed. The ability to force change. Right away, not at some unspecific time in the faraway future, but here and now. He'd left the earthold for exactly this reason, to be able to work with people who could make a difference, who could make things happen.

It wasn't long though, and he realized he'd been invited only to serve as the jester beside the king; an uneducated and presumably unwashed source of amusement. It had been a shock, but one he absorbed easily. He'd long ago hardened himself against the isolation and scorn of others.

As a child he was unpopular. Even now it took little to recall the taunting chorus; "Spud is a du-ud, spud is a du-ud!" Once, he'd thought he could change the things that set him apart; his name, his clothes, his speech.

"I want people to call me Tate," Potato complained, as he continued the hated job of pulling weed seedlings, "but you call me Potato, so everyone else does too."

A slight frown formed on his mother Radish's usually smiling face. "We don't use citinames here, dear," she replied. "We use names that remind us of our ties to the cycles of life and death." Her eyes were worried, almost fearful.

What does she have to be afraid of? Potato thought resentfully. She doesn't have to live with such a stupid name.

"And why food names?" he asked bitterly, "Why not something more... more dignified, more powerful?" As always, he felt each word displayed his apartness. Why did he never feel right, not even at home - with his own family, or in his study group, or cooperative?

"Potato," Radish reprimanded softly, "Dignity is found in usefulness. Our purpose is to return balance to the world – and not to seek power." Seeing his face remaining set in resistance, his mother shook her head slightly and added gently, "And darling, even if we do not seek power, there is no process so powerful as the web of sustenance that connects us all. Food is the most powerful force in the universe."

The corners of Potato's mouth remained bunched, but his eyes re-centered on hers. Something had caught his interest. "We chose the name Potato because it is such a useful food. It grows easily, it stores well ..." Radish trailed off. Potato's eyes were disinterested again.

Radish sighed and stepped onto the path leading to the dining hall. Then she turned back for a moment and said with reluctance, "I will call you 'Tater if you prefer it to Potato, but I will not call you Tate." And with a meaningful look she added firmly, "Our names remind us of our purpose. We are not citifolk who live their lives without direction or connection."

Eventually Tate realized it wasn't his name, but something in his character that made people see him as an oddity. Perhaps he would never fit anywhere, never be understood by anyone. Certainly Seth and his crowd had quickly decided he wasn't worthy of respect.

That's fine, he thought. Let them think me stupid. Maybe I will even appear a little deaf. I'll learn them, everything about them, and eventually … eventually perhaps I'll learn more than is safe for them.

He hid his anger and kept quiet. That had been easy. The times that he somehow attracted Seth's intense attention – were a little less easy, but in that first year, he worked hard to hide any discomfort and to prove himself reliable.

Then something – perhaps Tate's tolerance for being used as a joke, or a sex toy, or just the novelty of certain comments about life at the earthhold – prompted Seth to give Tate a residence within his own estate. Tate knew better than to consider that a reward. Seth just liked the convenience.

Seth had so many partners to select from that he didn't use Tate for sex often, and when he did, he was quite easily satisfied, and often generous for days afterward. In less than a year, Seth offered Tate his 'own' production laboratory and staff at Ocea Inc. in Bielefeld.

Tate had been careful to never request anything. So it made him a little uneasy to realize Seth had somehow seen him, known him well enough to guess a production lab would be a welcome gift.

"Do what you want," Seth said lazily as he drew a manicured hand across Tate's well-defined thigh. "I can write it off if it doesn't amount to anything, but just be sure to pass on anything useful. If you don't," he warned from lowered lids, "I'll find out. And it will be your ass." His gaze lingered meaningfully on the lower half of Tate's anatomy.

Tate managed not to react visibly, but his heart

quickened. Seth had only once turned their time together into a somewhat unpleasant experience, and Tate wasn't eager to receive another 'education in compliance.' Especially since he sensed that Seth's psyche contained a hidden core of sadism that he hadn't yet unleashed; at least not on Tate.

Running the production lab proved to be an incredible education of an entirely different kind. With Seth's carte blanche, Tate was able to bring virtually any useful person or tool to bear on his projects. He'd brought on one after another food scientist and statistician, and each revealed methods that were new to him. And while they used them only in the pursuit of developing an ever more efficient food product, Tate could see so many other applications.

It was a reminder to Tate of what he felt growing up, but was unable to put into words – earthold communities had fallen far behind in their scientific knowledge and skill. He'd so often been frustrated in his desire to learn not just what ecological relationships existed, but why and how. It seemed that Eartholders were becoming a self-limited people mulishly pursuing the same paths.

Do they know, do they understand back home what they are missing? Tate wondered. The power of knowledge … and then in that thought, Tate was cast back to a similar phrase, one that stayed with him from childhood, "there is nothing more powerful …" In an instant, the child's frustration, the adult's passion, and his enforced passivity at Seth's hands coalesced into a single idea … an idea that would not leave him in the coming months, and eventually transformed itself into a plan.

He felt a certain hidden terror at what he now intended to accomplish. And a part of him, equally suppressed wondered, was the impetus for his plan a desire to take revenge, to enact some kind of punishment on Seth? Or was it truly from a desire to salvage the eartholds and return them to viability? Did it matter, he wondered? If he could accomplish both at the same time, did the purity of his motives matter?

In the end, his inner thoughts made no difference. A visit back home to the earthold set events in motion. And Tate – the always impatient one – had begun a plan that would take years to reach fruition.

Seth surveyed himself in the mirrors of his dressing room. He practiced a powerful, but gracious smile. Hands smoothed down the flowing lines of his dull gold overdress. The black accents were understated; just faintly emphasizing the line where the garment parted in front as he walked. Smiling again at the impression he would make, he turned from the mirrors, walked away, then turned back and walked briskly, commandingly forward. The two sides of the overdress split as he strode and the brilliant orange-red radiance of his pants flashed within the opening. The effect was stunning.

From sedate and rather ordinary when standing or viewed from behind, his appearance became brilliant, flashy and yes, powerful when approaching. And should anyone forget that power, he had only to shift his stance when standing, or cross his legs when sitting and the flash of color would immediately convey a reminder.

Yes, Tate was continuing to prove himself an asset. His offhand mention of beetles that used warning colors to ward off birds had led to Seth's very satisfactory conference with his stylist, clothier and fabric supplier.

The crowd waiting for entrance to the latest Seth Stephen Sanger soiree was filled with excited voices and extravagant gestures – except from the handsome pair standing in line among the first dozen or so. They stood quietly together; the tall svelte female with a calm face, dark almond-shaped eyes and the olive skin of some southern clime, and the equally tall, angular, pale-skinned and midnight-black-haired male beside her.

They made an arresting couple, except that their body language didn't mark them as a couple. They could have been brother or sister perhaps. Her straight chestnut hair was only lightly restrained at the temples and then flowed like maple syrup behind her ears, over her shoulders and down to the small of her back. Her clothing was deceptively simple – a short tunic with translucent full sleeves, worn over tailored slacks. The lightweight fabric shifting with her movement revealed the long lean lines of her legs. The man's deep-set eyes revealed a little more interest in the crowd than hers, but he too stood quietly. His gray shirt and slacks were unusual among the usual male attire of black or navy. And in contrast to current styles, his hair was closely trimmed, forming a neat helmet that contrasted dramatically with the pale skin that reflected the streetlight.

As the line moved forward, the woman touched his sleeve to pause him, and said, "Jerome, a moment, please. I'll introduce you to Seth, but after that, I won't risk my position with him to show support for your proposal. You'll be on your own. So any questions, any advice; now's the time."

Jerome's eyebrows lowered on her in a frown, "What? But Lillian, you agree; it's important that we protect the exclosures, they're critical resources!"

Lillian nodded her head. "Yes, I agree. The Eartholders need our help. They just don't have the knowledge or resources to protect the exclosures, even if it is their responsibility. But you must understand that what matters most to Seth is control. His control. If he were at all uncertain about your project, my support would just infuriate him. And I can't lose the opportunity to try again with someone new if you don't succeed."

"You're so certain I'll fail?" Jerome asked, his tone rising. "Why introduce me then? This isn't a game to me, Lillian." He dropped his chin and his eyes became demanding. He lowered his voice, "If you're not serious, tell me now. I won't be a toy. Not his, and not yours."

Lillian's eyes twinkled and lit with genuine amusement. "Ah, Jerome… I said his control matters. I was through with toys ages ago." She took in his stony look and stepped nearer to say quietly, "I do believe in you. But Seth is volatile. Even if you play him exactly as I suggested, with no missteps, you still might not gain his support. And if he isn't interested, then you're done. Best to try again later with someone else's proposal. I can think of one or two others that might be attractive to him."

"Very well," Jerome replied, now calm again. "It makes no sense to me, but I'll do as you say. No direct invitations, no information offered until he asks; just complain about the job and drop a hint or two on what research changes have occurred."

"Exactly right. He's quite bright and very opportunistic, so if he's in the right mood he will ask those questions. And the less interested you act about his inquiries, the more confident he'll be that it's all his idea. He can pat himself on the back about how clever he is, and have something to brag about later," Lillian explained.

Jerome wrinkled his nose, "A bit odious, don't you think? Why'd you befriend him anyway?"

"Well," Lillian said dryly, "I wouldn't put it quite that way."

A month ago, Lillian had looked across the roomful of tables at the HighHundred Social, each one appearing as a single bloom with a handful of guests clustering like busy bees about its surface. They even sound like bees she mused. So sad that none of them would likely ever see a bee, hear the humming of its wings, or watch one push its way into a flower. She'd made a lengthy and somewhat inconvenient trip, and undergone two different decontamination procedures just to get into the exclosure that held one of the last wild populations of bumblebees. And, she thought grimly, as one of the guests caught her glance and began an oh-so-casual stalk in her direction, sometimes they sting like them too.

Seth smiled his insincere smile as he took her hand and patted it with imaginary affection. "I'm so pleased to see you here, my dear," he said.

Lillian presented her best insincere smile in return, but said nothing. Really, there was so little to say.

"I was so worried that our little disagreement might have made you feel too uncomfortable to appear in public. But here you are! I'm so pleased your... retirement, from society was short-lived."

Lillian smiled again, genuine amusement making it appear a little friendlier than she intended. So he'd thought her research trips were a retirement from society?

"Luckily," she replied somewhat dryly, "There were so many new concepts and theories generated by our associates at BioLabs-EastSydney, that I was kept busy creating new models for proposed research studies." Inwardly Lillian smiled again. She could almost see Seth's energy levels drop, and his gaze was already floating about the room.

"Yes?" he murmured, "Well, I'm so happy that you are able to immerse yourself in work, my dear. As for myself, I have other interests." And with another tight smile he released her hand and sauntered off in the direction of the float-floor where couples and even a few triples were undulating under the influence of the music set to produce pheromones at unexpected moments.

"Really, Lil – I don't know why you keep discouraging Seth," a voice at her elbow whispered. "He's really very eligible."

Lillian turned and took in her friend's mischievous grin. The petite Afrikaan's dimples were showing and her gilded braids bobbed and glistened as she lowered and tilted her chin.

"Carla! When did you come in? I was so glad to hear you'd be back in time for the Social," Lillian said delightedly.

"Just a few minutes ago," Carla said with a grin, "Was a little surprised to see Seth with you after all the grousing you did."

"Oh, forget him – tell me what you've been up to!" Lillian said smiling.

Carla smiled back and responded, "I've been getting

married."

"What? Don't tell me you finally gave in to family pressure. I thought you and I were going to hold out against all influences and find matches for reasons other than politics, company holdings or even business acumen."

"Well, as it happens, I think I have. Now grab something solid sweetie – I went and married an Eartholder. He's a scientist... but still, it's going to be tough going for him if we try to live within SNN. So, I may just commute."

"Oh my," Lillian replied. Carla had always enjoyed swimming upstream. Lillian was less of a thrill-seeker, but would fight the currents if necessary – as it often was to pursue her obsession with science rather than business. But to marry an Eartholder ... that was truly embracing risk.

"Well, you'll have to introduce me," Lillian replied.

Carla laughed, "Oh yes, most certainly. You'll enjoy him. I think."

The increasing murmur in the reception room restored Tate's attention; Seth must be making his entrance.

Seth strode forward; pleased with the way people parted in front of him, the widened eyes and exclamations of surprise demonstrating how effectively his garments spoke for him. He flashed orange-red with each step and then, when he reached the center of the room, he stopped. The dull gold of his overcoat draped gently down and he became a subdued golden column. Understated. Elegant. He allowed a single small smile to appear – and the crowd surged forward, offering compliments, asking questions, paying homage.

Tate watched attentively as Seth all but glowed. If the evening continued as it started, Seth would be stoked and eager to work the adrenaline off with one or more of his partners tonight. But Tate could worry about that later. For now, he'd just keep an unobtrusive presence, and survey the guests – the odd remark in overheard conversations on nights like these often pointed the way to a new resource.

Lillian suppressed an urge to clap ironically as Seth commanded the room's attention with his entrance. Well, she thought, at least he'll be approachable this evening. Beside her, Jerome watched people vie for space and time around Seth Stephen Sanger, the man the media referred to as TripleS – a nickname the temporary blogs gleefully expanded to TripleShit. Even if Lillian gets thru that mess and introduces me, what can I say to capture his attention, Jerome worried, especially if I can't be direct?

Lillian casually led Jerome through a series of introductions to some of the smaller production powers in the room, while watching Seth's movements. Yes, Seth was using the evening to reconnect with his grant recipients. To approach Seth too soon might appear too eager; too needy. The more unintentional it seemed, the better.

"Any idea why Seth wanted us here tonight?" Frank Putnam asked the production manager standing beside him.

"No idea. Maybe it's just a reward for good behavior," Marie Cargill offered with a sideways smile.

"Well these 'crab cakes' are no reward," replied Putnam, "They're just as boring as they were the first two hundred times we've had them. Do you think there's any crab in them?"

"Oh, be fair," Cargill laughed, and grinned, "They weren't boring the first three or four times."

"Speaking of boring," Putnam began.

"Oh, I know what you're going to say," Cargill interjected.

"If we don't get a new product line to play with soon I'm going to lose the last brain cells I have," Putnam finished.

"Don't even start," Cargill growled, "Just yesterday I got word that it's going to get worse."

"What? How could it?" Putnam asked.

"I saw the preview of a 'vert proclaiming that SNN citizens will have an opportunity to select a new combo with their next nutrient order. It will combine all the nutrients from MorningBuzz and JoyJuice. So you know what that means," Cargill said.

"Oh no," Putnam groaned. "They'll phase out JoyJuice and MorningBuzz and we'll be down to just one breakfast drink. The job is going to get even more boring."

Cargill frowned and looked around to see if anyone was in listening distance and then said in very soft tones, "Worse than that, you can bet we'll be asked which of our staff can be dispensed with – and it might not be much longer and you and I will be in the same situation."

"All in the name of more efficient nutrient production," Putnam said bitterly.

"Don't be naïve, Frank," Cargill said soberly, "It's all in the name of more profit." Then as she noted Seth moving out of the crowd and strolling nearer, she whispered, "Proximity alert, shields on maximum."

Lillian watched as one of Seth's lovers moved from his position at the side of the crowd to join a pair of production managers, and then she touched Jerome's elbow and gathered him with a look … they might just be able to arrange for Seth to approach them. A slow stroll took Jerome and her to the threesome.

"Frank, Marie," Lillian said with a gentle smile, "And, Tate isn't it? Did any of you hear where Seth got that glorious material? It has a very subtle shimmer to it."

"Ah, no," Marie Cargill replied, "We were just beginning to wonder where the new creative genius is – do you think Seth has him locked up in a room somewhere?"

"Hmmm, like Rumplestiltskin – spinning gold?" Lillian replied with a laugh. "Possible, highly possible."

Jerome nodded politely at all three, but involuntarily ran his eyes over the man Lillian had addressed as Tate. The man could have stepped out from within a Michelangelo statue – the silver clothing did nothing to hide, and everything to reveal a classically beautiful body. The thin silk turtleneck was shot with subtle vertical lines of silver thread that emphasized every bump and ridge of muscle that undulated along ribcage, chest and arms, and the dull silver jeans fit him more like tights than trousers. Jerome saw the muscles in those legs bunch and shift and self-consciously jerked his eyes abruptly back to the man's face. Luckily Tate had been looking at Lillian, and Jerome narrowed his eyes as he realized that something indefinable set the man apart as an Eartholder. Perhaps it was the dark, yet uneven tan, with an almost leathery appearance. It wasn't the hair – most Eartholders cropped their hair in a utilitarian cut, but Tate's fell in soft-looking brown layers to the top of his shoulders.

Tate gazed consideringly at Lillian, and then at the rather arrestingly handsome man accompanying her. She usually avoided Seth and anyone close to him – what was she up to?

A short distance away, Seth was thinking how pleasant it was that Lillian was here tonight. Not that he he'd changed his mind about joining their respective empires; she was clearly not as suitable as someone less unconventional - but it couldn't hurt for her to see one of his most effective soirees and reflect on what she was missing. She'd sometimes seemed, not reluctant, of course not... but perhaps a little less eager to pursue the prospect of matrimony than expected.

Seth smiled and stepped forward to join the group. "And how are you enjoying the evening? Are the refreshments satisfying?" he asked.

'As always, Seth, as always, they are delightful," Frank replied ingratiatingly.

"I'm pleased of course that you are pleased," Seth replied. "However, I personally find a little monotony in the appetizers, and have wondered if it is time to find a new chef."

Jerome's eyes widened slightly and his mouth parted; this could be the opening he'd hoped for, but was distracted as Lillian turned abruptly, and bumped against him.

"Oh, my apologies, Jerome. I'm so clumsy. I just saw an old lab partner across the room and must go say hi. Oh, goodness, and I completely forgot to introduce you. Jerome, Jerome Kirkland ... please meet Marie Cargill of C3D Inc., Frank Putnam of Kelpco, Tate ... oh sorry, Tate I'm not sure I caught your family name... of Ocea Inc. and of course Seth Stephen Sanger, our host. As I'm sure you know, he funds the lot of them, and likely half the room for that matter, with his suite of research grants to encourage production innovation. I'm sure you'll find that you have a lot in common. Now I must run. I'll catch up with you later, alright?!" Lillian said with a deliberately distracted smile and then whisked herself off.

Jerome smiled a little self-consciously and offered handshakes all around. Marie's was firm, Frank's perfunctory, and Tate's... a rather direct look accompanied his handshake, and as their hands and eyes met Jerome was aware of an unusual tingle. Seth Sanger took his hand in an unnecessarily strong grip, then released it, smiled and said, "And what brings you here to our little party? Are you Lillian's new toy?"

A slight flush appeared on Jerome's cheeks. "No, not at all – although I'm sure that would be pleasant. We became acquainted at East Sydney when she visited BioLabs to discuss new models. I mentioned I was planning a visit here, and she offered to show me around."

"Ah, BioLabs ... you do research there, don't you? Pure science stuff?" Seth's tone was dry and dismissive.

"Well of course that's the company's history. Lately though..." Jerome released a sigh that he hoped seemed sincere, "Lately they've got us running series after series after series, just varying an ingredient here and there, and now the sommeliers they hired last year seem to have more pull on what research gets funded than any of the proposals we've submitted. Frustrating, that's what it is."

"Sommeliers?" Seth inquired gently from hooded eyes.

"Yes, as if wine tasters would know more about food chemistry than we would? I mean, c'mon, if we were producing wine – but we're supposed to be a research facility." Jerome commented as bitterly as possible.

"Hmmm. Perhaps management is looking to branch out?" Seth inquired, even more casually, and with his gaze casually surveying the crowd as if the answer was of no importance.

"Who knows? All I know is the research I've been trying to get moved up for years is being sidelined by whatever new bee has gotten into management's bonnet," Jerome replied and then thought, So far, so good. If Lillian's assessment of Seth is correct, he'll want to know exactly what research is going on.

"It's a common problem," Frank interjected. "Even those of us in applied research sometimes have our projects derailed by the next great idea," he added. And then as Seth's eyebrow rose he flushed and added hastily, "Of course sometimes the next great idea is actually a brilliant idea – and a money maker that funds all our future projects."

Seth's eyebrow remained upraised and he tilted his head slightly without taking his eyes away from Frank's.

Frank's Adam's apple bobbed and he cleared his throat, "Naturally, the most important- "

"I think you've said enough," Seth interrupted. "Silence might be the better choice at this juncture."

Seth then turned to Jerome and said with a suddenly charismatic smile, "You should tell me about your project, the one you've been trying to get moved up? I'm sure that it is quite full of brilliant ideas, and I think some new funding may become available as we… reduce staffing a bit in other areas."

Tate watched as Seth laid an arm around Jerome's shoulders and led him off toward the chairs near the buffet tables. He frowned as he noted how well they looked together, both lithe and moving smoothly; Seth's golden hair tied in a loose queue at the back and Jerome's hair a dark sheen of black satin tapered neatly to his strong neck. That was quick, he thought. Was that Lillian's purpose? To put Jerome in Seth's path? And if so, why? Tate's eyes searched for Lillian in the crowd. She was standing against a wall, also watching Seth and Jerome's progress toward the tables.

"Hello, Lillian," Tate said and handed her a flute of Seth's latest beverage of choice. He took a small sip from his own glass.

"Tate – I didn't see you coming. Thank you," Lillian replied and then cast a questioning gaze upon him.

"We don't see you much at casual events like these," Tate commented.

"No ... I'm afraid I really prefer research, but sometimes a break is called for," Lillian explained.

"Hmmm," Tate returned noncommittally. "Your friend, Jerome? He seems to have attracted Seth's attention."

"Yes? Well, that's interesting; Seth is always bored when I talk research," Lillian smiled.

"Does Jerome swing that way?" Tate asked bluntly.

Lillian's eyes swung up to his in surprise. "You think Seth is attracted to him physically? Oh, blast, I hadn't thought of that."

"But you did think of introducing them," Tate said darkly.

Lillian tilted her head and looked more closely at Tate. He was always so very quiet – and she'd assumed that he was disengaged as well. "I'm sorry," she said, "Are you worried about Seth transferring his attentions? I rather doubt Seth is interested in Jerome that way. It's more likely they've found something of interest to talk about, don't you think?"

Tate frowned again and then reluctantly, lowered his voice and said quietly, "If Seth is interested, and Jerome's not... you'll warn him not to reject Seth, won't you? People who displease him tend to have difficulty resuming successful lives." Tate paused and then added, "Jerome's best bet will be to have reason to be called away. To somewhere too inconvenient for Seth to bother searching him out."

Lillian's surprise was written across her face. Tate was a lot more than he appeared.

Tate scowled and tossed off the last of his glass and added, "Just saying. No skin off my nose." As he strode off,

Tate wondered where the hell his warning had come from. Jerome Kirkland was citifolk, a SNN lifelong citizen, and likely much more comfortable moving among the HighHundred than Tate would ever be. Tate found himself wondering if he was jealous. If so, he would just have to adjust his thinking. Seth was a tool, nothing more.

Tate uneasily reminded himself to keep such thoughts well below the surface. If Seth ever discovered that Tate had used his funding and facilities to prepare the way for Seth's own destruction... Luckily, hardly anyone visited Bielefeld, and even if they did, the lab supported dozens of different research projects, and almost all of them were unknown to each other since the facilities were essentially rented out. Nonetheless, it might not hurt to make certain Coriander's cover story was secure.

The lab at Ocea Inc. was right in the center of Bielefeld just off of Jahnplatz, but much like the city itself, in spite of a regular stream of workers coming and going each day on the moBiel, it somehow maintained an insubstantial presence. It was just one building sandwiched among all the others, and when Tate first led her there, Coriander was unsure she'd find it easily again.

Quickly though, the commute from the earthold became routine, even if the work was not. It took weeks for Coriander to feel comfortable closed in on all sides by walls without windows; to use the clock to measure the day's passing instead of the movements of the birds or the sun. Those things were harder to remember than Tate's caution to tell no one what she was raising, or why.

"If any one asks, Cory – just say you've been told to duplicate previous trials. Nobody cares about work someone else has already done. And don't use the lab line to call Branch or Sandburr – use your personal phone – it's why I got you one," Tate said. He looked vaguely worried and Coriander smiled. People at home might say that Tate wasn't very friendly or helpful – but they just didn't know him. Sure he was mostly quiet, and he only really cared about things most people didn't care about. But she knew her big brother did care about her, and his worried frown was rare evidence of it. She'd missed him that first year after he'd left earthome, but this last year and a half since she'd come to the lab, they'd seen each other more often, even if it was to just share a progress report and perhaps split a Lieferheld pizza.

Coriander peered into the viewer, and carefully adjusted the NutriFlo's drip rate up by just one unit. It seemed wicked to keep withholding food – leaving them in a constant state of near starvation. But the sea skater nymphs were at that delicate stage where too much nutrient would cause them to split their skins before their legs were properly developed, and too little would deplete their reserve of lipids.

She reminded herself of the disastrous week when she'd foolishly added too much nutrient. Almost half of the nymphs died from split skins that exposed their internal organs to the drying air. The rest were so engorged they were unable to maneuver; thank goodness they were in the lab where there were no predators. Coriander winced again as she remembered the setbacks her lapse in control had caused, and resolutely steeled herself to ignore the empathy that made it hard to limit their food.

It was easier to distract herself with work, so she set control sequences to run the current dataset with all the common measures against their models; population, weights, rate of development, nutrient consumption, and hatch to mortality ratio estimates. It was a good hour and a half early, so it would only be preliminary data, but it might give her a few hints on where she should focus her analysis when she ran the final regularly scheduled report.

Coriander wrinkled her nose and highlighted the total population section of her prelim report, and then brought onscreen last week's hatch report and highlighted the same section. She shook her head. On both reports she'd also compared nutrient levels, developmental stages, temperature and space constraints; everything was nearly identical, except total population. How could that be? This was prelim data, but still, how could this population be double the prior hatch? It should be impossible. An incremental increase might be explained by improved breeding success by those in the population that were better adapted to the environmental conditions, but a two-fold increase?

For the second time Coriander checked every setting on the equipment. Again she could find nothing wrong. How were they sustaining themselves on nutrients that should have been enough for just half their number?

She ran a hand through her hair, still vaguely missing the less fashionable but shorter crop she'd taken for granted at the earthold. She started nervously at the buzz of the ReportMinder, then hugged herself briefly before entering the final control sequences to run the regularly scheduled dataset.

Her hand trembled a little as she pressed 'begin.' Surely her two preliminary runs were flukes. Perhaps she'd caught the Halobates' population at the moment prior to a die-off adjustment to nutrient levels. Or perhaps... a ding indicated report completion. Coriander stopped musing and leaned in to read the results. And then pressed her fingers to her mouth - population increase 278.37513% +- .18236. Coriander pulled out her phone.

Sandburr wrestled his phone out of his overalls pocket and separated it from the usual deposits of feathers, seeds, leaves and other collected items that seemed to go from his hand to his pocket without conscious thought during the day. The smile that hadn't left his face since his wedding last month did fade a little as he read Coriander's somewhat cryptic text. Pop ^278.37+%. Reason unk. Need invest. Sorry.

The 'sorry' was probably for interrupting his honeymoon. She couldn't know that his wife - wow, love that; wife - had decided to take a quick daytrip to attend the HighHundred Social; 'to brag about you, sweetie, to my bff.' That did leave him free to take a look at Coriander's question, although he'd been enjoying his day in the field. If she was referring to a population increase in the latest Halobates hatch – that was just crazy. She'd probably messed up the nutro, but... he hadn't visited SNN for a while. He could make a quick visit and maybe even surprise Carla with an overnight stay.

The grin returned full-force. Sandburr texted a quick response, gathered his collection bottles, loupe, tweezers and other tools, threw them in his pail, and began working his way back through the shrubs and grasses to where he'd parked his three-wheel.

The café was doing an excellent business, and was filled with the noise of people chatting, pots ringing in the kitchen, and chairs pushed in or pulled back as one table emptied and another was seated. Jerome realized he was sitting a little forward on his chair, and repositioned himself to lean against the back. He might be a little anxious, but it couldn't help to appear that way. Moments later Seth and Tate approached the table. Seth was looking annoyed and Tate... Tate was as quiet and self-contained as he'd been at Seth's soiree. Jerome couldn't help but notice that Tate's mustard colored shirt clung to him. Was the tight clothing a personal preference, Jerome wondered, or something Seth commanded? He'd learned from Seth's not-so-subtle conversation the night of the soiree, that Tate was something more than a research grantee.

"Mr. Kirkland," Seth greeted him frigidly.

"Sir, did you have difficulty getting through the crowd?" Jerome asked warmly, "I'm so sorry, I did ask the host to watch for you and bring you in right away – but they are so swamped he must have missed you. I do apologize – but I promise the meal will be worth it,"

Seth did not respond, but seemed slightly mollified by Jerome's apology, and more so when a waiter appeared and poured him a cordial.

"I hope you won't think me impertinent, but I asked your

house staff to send a bottle of your favorite over so you could have exactly what you like best to drink – they don't serve alcoholic beverages here yet; some difficulty in getting a license I take it," Jerome added.

Seth leaned back, took a sip and offered a stiff smile, "Well, I trust the meal will be something special – and that you can explain to Tate precisely why he ought to allow you to work with him on a new product line."

"Tate – I'm pleased … it's good to see you again," Jerome managed to say. Something about the man's intent gaze made him feel oddly restless. It wasn't unpleasant, and in fact somewhat warming to be at the center of his attention, but it was a little distracting. He couldn't quite keep his eyes off Tate's hands; they looked incredibly strong, and tough and work-worn.

The meal finished, and Seth having departed after issuing one of his terse instructions to Tate, 'Hire him, or fund him or whatever the hell works – but I want these products for my next event,' Jerome was awaiting Tate's response.

Tate leveled yet another of those oddly penetrating gazes on Jerome and then passed him the dish of salted almonds. He liked Jerome's looks – the dark eyes seemed so honest, and his lean angular body was attractive compared to the soft … Tate cut the thought off. He wasn't free to consider anything of a personal nature. He waited until Jerome had selected and bitten into one of the almonds before asking softly, "So you would like to research a series of product lines that would provide less efficient nutrition, and offer it for sale at higher prices than current nutrient offerings – and you expect that to be profitable?"

Jerome chewed madly, wondering if he'd timed that deliberately, and then took a sip of water. So, he wants to play power games? Ok, I can do that.

With as little expression as possible, Jerome countered with, "Then it doesn't matter that Seth just told you to fund me – you're prepared to turn me down? How do you plan to explain that?"

Tate almost laughed. Jerome was ridiculously easy to read. He was willing to try to play the game, but didn't have a clue how.

Jerome relaxed as something in him recognized that Tate, for whatever reason, liked him.

"Look, Tate – I think I can be perfectly honest with you," Jerome said earnestly and leaned forward to bring their gazes closer together. "I really don't care about the products, or the profit - or Seth's next event for that matter. Those are all just a means to an end. What I do care about, what will motivate me to help you satisfy that egomaniac, is finding a way to make the last remaining natural environments relevant and profitable so that they don't all get destroyed.

"There are very few of them, of the exclosures, that aren't threatened by all kinds of things, but especially by the encroachment of trashlands. Any scientist who can call himself one knows that if we can't stop that from happening - well, global warming changed everything – but if the exclusions, the eartholds, are lost, it will end everything," Jerome said fervently, "We may as well all load into a ship headed straight into the sun, because we're dead, all of us. Dead."

Tate stared at the sincere eyes, unable to believe the naiveté; the sheer idiocy of the man. Didn't he realize that a single word to Seth … where the hell did he get off trusting Tate that way!

"You are an idiot." The words left Tate's mouth without volition, and immediately he flushed as he realized that for the second time in as many weeks, he'd spoken without thinking. "Look, you just can't go around talking about Seth like that to people you don't know; you'll find yourself... I don't know why I care but there are more trashlands all the time; do you want to end up in one?" What is it about this man that makes me think I should protect him, Tate wondered.

Jerome grinned. "Tate, I appreciate the warning, but hey,

I have great instincts – and they're telling me that Seth may think he owns you, but you know better. Am I right? So, let's forget about him for a while, and let's talk production. To answer your first question, yes I do think we can offer production lines with lower nutrition and higher cost and be profitable; in fact very, very profitable. People are bored with their limited food and beverage choices. They'll pay more, a lot more, for something that can provide more satisfaction. Have you ever heard about the studies done by Howard Moskowitz? This guy showed that you can measure people's taste preferences so accurately that they can be used to tweak production recipes until a food achieves its 'bliss point'. Then this got taken to the next logical step; foods were actually designed to be addictive. Before we all got so absorbed with managing the consequences of global warming, there were movements starting that were trying to make 'addictive foods' illegal!"

Tate listened and watched and wondered. Jerome trusted Tate. Could Tate trust Jerome? If he succeeded in wresting power from Seth, might there be some other future possible?

Sandburr leaned back in the lab chair, clasped both hands behind his head and rubbed them back and forth across his nubby salt and pepper hair. Coriander stood watching him as patiently as possible, saying nothing, but when he continued to simply stare into space she sat down, put a finger to her mouth, and began worrying at the cuticle.

"Yer momma would douse that with pickle juice, she saw you eatin' at your finger like that," Sandburr rumbled.

Coriander pulled her finger away and sat up straighter on her stool, "Did… did you find anything wrong in my runs?"

"Girl, you worry too much about yourself," Sandburr replied.

"Please Burr, did I mess up? Or is the hatch really… " she trailed off, still unwilling to put into words the numbers from her reports.

"Coriander honey, you did just fine. And you were right

to text me. We have ourselves something a little special here," Sandburr replied slowly.

Coriander took a breath and then let it out slowly and whispered, "A mutation ... a mutation?"

Sandburr looked over at her, at the wide eyes and the mix of hope and fear and said solemnly, "That's right, sweetie. And that changes everything."

Branch could feel his breath struggling to stay even, battling the adrenaline as Eartholders filed into the meeting hall. Even though he'd had several days and nights to absorb and reflect on Sandburr's astonishing news, it was still unreal to him. It was tempting to imagine Mother Earth herself had decided to lend a hand to aid them. And just as easy to imagine Trickster, playing his games – challenging their resolve to take only the correct actions, and not the easy path. He must remember, they all must remember, that a misstep could lead to the destruction of everything they were trying to protect.

The small room was nearly full; Sandburr was at one of the tables off to the right and beside him was a vivacious but elegant lady whose bright eyes seemed to dart everywhere, taking everything in as if she'd never seen anything like it before. With each turn of her head, the braids falling from her cornrows tossed and the tiny golden threads woven into them caught the light and sparkled.

On the other side of the room, nearer to the front, Coriander sat with an older couple, and the three of them patiently watched the front of the room where Tate stood immobile. Tate's appearance would never be dramatic; his ordinary brown hair and eyes, average build and quiet personality ensured that. But he'd made an effort to display himself to advantage; his cream shirt and chocolate brown jacket and slacks were tailored, and his hair was cut more stylishly than the last time Coriander had seen him.

As the last few walked in silently and found their seats, Branch sent a meaningful glance in Tate's direction and then closed both heavy doors.

Tate took a few steps forward and standing on the balls of his feet, raised his voice to carry to the back of the room, "Everyone, everyone – thank you for coming."

"Decades ago with the creation of the very first Exclusion, we Eartholders took on the responsibility, the dedicated purpose, to keep safe, healthy and intact the last greatest and most diverse places on earth; to preserve these last lands where ecological interconnections keep all living things in balance."

"But our purpose is in jeopardy."

"Why? Do we lack the will to protect our eartholds?"

"No! We lack the power to protect them."

"Twenty years ago our earthold was cocooned with buffering farms and fallow lands spun around it for a hundred miles in every direction. Just three years ago, when I asked you to listen to my proposal, within twenty miles there were two financially struggling farms, three abandoned farmsteads, and four trashlands. You couldn't go fifty miles in any direction without running into a significant disturbance to the natural ecosystems."

"Today? Those four trashlands have expanded in size so they're now within 18 miles of our earthold. A fifth trashland is being built twenty-two miles to our south. The two farms haven't been sold – yet – but both are in talks with their creditors. And one of those abandoned farmsteads has already been sold – to yet another trashland developer."

"Now, we are half-encircled by trashlands."

"Why? Because we have no power to prevent it!"

Tate let his words sink into the quiet of the room. Then, with the first few signs of restlessness he resumed, "We all see a terrible future ahead of us if we do nothing; a future where the entire world is engineered for efficiency and profit and the natural world no longer exists."

Tate's jaw clenched and he turned an angry gaze on the crowd and said firmly, "Three years ago we all agreed that the only way Eartholders could keep their promise to protect the eartholds was to take power. And I proposed a plan to do that."

"We didn't all agree to that plan. But we did all agree to pursue the research, and take the preliminary steps needed to carry it out - and to meet again when we'd reached a point where it could be implemented."

"That day is today. It is time for us to decide; do we have the will to do what we can, to take the power to protect the eartholds, to fulfill our promises?"

As Tate gestured for Branch to come forward, the room filled with murmurs, sounds of fear and hope and suppressed excitement. As Branch walked around the tables to the front Tate raised his voice again over the sounds of people's whispered conversations to say loudly, "I'm not much of a leader of people," and as the voices quieted he added, "and a project like this, requires a leader; someone we can trust, with integrity, and compassion, but also patience and dedication. We chose Branch to be that leader. Branch, thank you. Can you please fill everyone in on what's been accomplished?"

Branch looked around the room with an easy smile, and as always, people immediately quieted and sat a little straighter in their chairs. Branch spoke into the silence, "I'll tell you first about the Sea Skater Breeding Project. But, since we didn't all agree that was the right direction to go, I asked some of you to help me explore some other ideas. I'll tell you all a little more about that later."

"For now, let's just remind ourselves that the basic idea behind Tate's proposal was that we take advantage of SNNs weaknesses, and our own strengths, to gain enough power to protect the eartholds. And their major weakness is an almost complete reliance on a single food source, zooplankton, and a uniform method to produce and distribute that food."

A small gasp came from somewhere in the room, and as heads turned to look about them, Sandburr took the hand of the elegant lady next to him and pressed it reassuringly. He bent his big head down to press a kiss on the top of her nose and intoned, "Hold tight, Carla. Might be a bumpy ride; but you like that." Carla looked at him reprovingly and tossed her head, braids swinging to slap at her neck, but in the next instant deep dimples appeared in her cheeks.

"Hey, hey – yeah girl, that's right – you're safe with me," Sandburr said with a chuckle.

Branch cleared his throat and said, "Yes, we had a few arguments about that, didn't we? None of us liked the idea of attacking world food production. We Eartholders like to think that we're dedicated to preserving life. But really, that's not quite right, is it? Really, we're dedicated to preserving the diversity of life. That means an ecosystem that includes not only life, but death. It's the complexity of relationships and the balance among them that's so important. There is not just one bee or beetle or ant for a single plant, but hundreds, thousands maybe. Not just one type of plant that an insect, or bat, or mouse can take nourishment from. Not just one predator, not just one prey. It's diversity that ensures the whole system can recover when there's too much of anything - or too little; rain, drought, fire, flood or disease."

Branch tilted his head at the crowd and spread the fingers of his hands out by his side as he said, "Some have argued – Tate, Sandburr, and others who've seen it firsthand – that the system of producing food within SNN is already unstable. That it's just a matter of time before a catastrophe occurs."

Branch shrugged his shoulders and his eyes smiled out at this person, and that person, and another across the room. "Perhaps that's true, but even so, that doesn't mean that we don't still need to act responsibly, morally."

"As far as our strengths go; I've already talked about them. We Eartholders understand that everything is connected. We know that diversity is healthy, that uniformity is not."

Branch stood for a moment eyeing the crowd, and then strode to the side of the room, grabbed a chair and hauled it back to the center, where he turned it round backwards and then sat on it tilted forward with his legs straddling it.

"So, that was the idea; we use a biological tool that will

create difficulties for the zooplankton that the HighHundred's production companies use as the building block for all of their food production."

"One of our challenges was that whatever tool we used, we needed it to be self-limiting if it escaped the food production lab sites, or at least have no negative effect to the oceanic ecology. We thought about breeding siphonophores; they're really cool animals and can do a lot of damage to zooplankton since they are highly mobile. But they were really too adaptable; there was no easy way to limit them if they escaped the labs. We also considered a virus or parasite, but again, a virus might be too adaptable, and a parasite depends on its host organism, and couldn't be expected to completely destroy the zooplankton."

"But sea skaters - Halobates - are limited to the surface of the ocean; the area referred to as the air/water interface. They don't dive, or fly, and in the natural world would never be a danger to the entire zooplankton population, because they can feed only on the plankton that is near the water's surface."

"And that makes them a perfect tool. In the food production labs, zooplankton are raised and harvested in shallow vats that are lined with sieves that are raised or lowered to harvest specific sizes of zooplankton, which provides sea skaters with an ideal feeding, breeding and hatching ground. The shallow vats keep plankton within reach of the sea skaters, and the sieves and vat sides are perfect surfaces for the adult sea skaters to lay their eggs. And lab temperature and humidity levels are kept within the optimum range for egg hatching."

"For the Sea Skater Breeding Project we selected Halobates sericeus to breed, and created models based on its known characteristics. Sandburr created these first models, but he felt they were too crude, and contracted for more complex models that could do a better job of predicting results."

"Tonight we have with us Carla-James Behnke who

created those final models. She's here today with her new husband - well, new as of about a month ago - Sandburr. So if people have questions about that - the models, not their marriage - then she can probably answer them later tonight."

Branch paused while the crowd smiled and laughed and twisted around to get a look at Carla.

"So, Carla's models tested conditions that we expected eggs, nymphs and adults to encounter. This helped us figure out what total population numbers we would need to significantly impact zooplankton production. We thought it would take three to four years to breed enough sea skaters."

"The reason we're all here tonight is because something unexpected happened. Sandburr – can you come up and tell people about that?"

Sandburr stood and turned his broad brown face to the room and said, "No need to go up there. In last week's hatch there was a mutation we didn't plan for within the population. Halobate sericeus nymphs and adults have always had the ability to store food reserves – lipids – that let them withstand periods of starvation; that's one of the reasons we selected that species. We wanted them to be able to survive relatively long periods without nutrient while we transported them.

"This mutation adds a different capability to increase species survival. They now have the ability to selectively hibernate some body functions and not others. For example, when they've captured prey, they can hibernate the body parts that are for locomotion - legs and so forth - while the rest of their functions - eating, digesting, etcetera - remain active. And when they are converting energy into physical development, such as molting or reproduction, then the body parts for chewing, and digestion hibernate. This hibernating function conserves energy, so the Halobates require less food to progress through all their life stages. The end result is that they're at least twice as efficient and can be bred at an accelerated rate, on less nutrient," Sandburr finished and sat back down.

Branch looked around the room, listening to the buzz as people began to react to that news. Then he unwrapped himself from the chair, and standing up, spread his arms out and appealed to his audience, "Folks, I know you all have questions, and we will talk things over later. Remember too, I still want to tell you about other ideas we're exploring."

"But now Carla, would you like to share what you think this will mean in terms of your models?"

Next to Sandburr, Carla stood and said, "Hello everyone. I won't make the mistake with you that I made with Sandburr, and assume you wouldn't know a statistical model from a runway model, but I must make a disclaimer; statistical models are really only guesses about what can happen. They can be really, really good guesses, since they're based on statistics and test results, but," and Carla paused and grinned at Sandburr mischievously, "they don't let us become gods, and create the future that we want. That said, I'm afraid I'm now going to disappoint everyone who thought that we'd have enough sea skaters to implement the plan in just a week or two."

As murmurs rose louder from the crowd, Sandburr began to glare and rise from his chair.

"Down boy," Carla said with a laugh and halted his rise with one slim hand on a shoulder. "You see everyone, my models were based on the characteristics of the sea skaters before they mutated. So while we might have enough sea skaters, we don't know quite enough about them – and we'll need to retest, to get a new set of stats that we can use to recalibrate the predictive models. And on top of that, since these critters have mutated, I would really like to get another statistician – a very good one – to help us make sure we've included all the data that is advisable with a mutated species. I just don't have any experience with mutated species." With that, Carla regained her seat.

"Okay, thanks Carla," Branch said, "I'll just add that three years ago, I contacted all of the other eartholds to see if any of them had thoughts about holding back the advances of the

trashlands, or increasing our influence within SNN. A few –
especially those with a larger proportion of inter-societal
marriages like Sandburr and Carla's – said that some citifolk
within SNN are supportive not only of protecting eartholds,
but also for expanding their ranges to include buffering
aglands, or nonproductive farmsteads. And a few mentioned
that the Eartholders who can tolerate a citifolk lifestyle are
usually very successful and highly valued within SNN
universities and research facilities. Their unique perspectives
help them see problems and solutions that elude their citibred
colleagues; and that also leads to broader support for
eartholds. However, very few Eartholders have been
interested in pursuing careers within SNN."

"So that led Sandburr and I to see what could be done to
build some alliances, friendships, and sympathetic
relationships, not just among other Eartholder communities,
but also among people within SNN who do consider
eartholds valuable."

"While we haven't yet achieved any changes in
regulations, we have determined that about one out of eight
citifolk do support increased earthold protections. While that
isn't nearly half, we also know that most of these folks have
jobs with influence. They tend to be the scientists or lab
workers who don't own or direct company operations, but do
make suggestions and propose changes. Also, we've
sponsored scholarships for Eartholder studygroup graduates
with an interest in attending research universities within
SNN."

"I think that just about covers everything. So, let's break
into groups for discussion, and then get back together in 10
minutes. Thank you!"

Tate folded his hands behind his back and stared at the
floor. He hated waiting, and they were so close, but he knew
he could not make this decision alone.

Lillian heard the distinctive tones of Carla's ring on her
phone, and flipped it open, "Carla! Hey sweetie, what's up?"

Lillian asked, leaning against the corridor wall.

"Can you meet me at Ocea Inc.'s lab in Bielefeld? I want to show you something and offer you a contract," Carla said.

"For you, I'll do it, though I'm up to my eyeballs. This afternoon?" Lillian offered.

"Careful. You might not like this one. It's a spooky – but I need someone good – and that's you. So at two then," Carla finished.

"So, watcha think?" Carla asked. Her tone was casual but her normally expressive hands were clenched tightly on her lap.

"Oh my god, Carla," Lillian breathed. She turned stunned eyes on her friend. "This is ..."

"I'm sorry. I know it's a lot to ask, but we must have a model that takes the mutation into account. I know you're sympathetic to Eartholders; you've been to more exclusion sites than I have. We've talked ..."

"Whoa – whoa, girl," Lillian interrupted. "You're right, I am sympathetic. More than you know. But this is the wrong way to go about fixing things. You said Sandburr called it a game changer and he's right, but not because the population levels can be reached faster – it's because with a mutation you have to start over from scratch and learn that organism all over again. You have to throw out everything you thought you knew about the previous organism. Without that, you can't create a model to predict with any accuracy what will happen."

"But Lil- " Carla began.

"No – listen Carla. I had no idea how interested – how invested - you'd become in the eartholds. But now that I know, you should know that I and some friends and colleagues have been working on this same problem, but from a different angle. To be blunt, from a more rational and less terroristic angle," Lillian said seriously.

Carla's eyes widened and brightened and her hands flew up in the air for a moment, and then she clasped them back together and drew them down to her lap. "Lillian MacMillan! Tell me!" she demanded.

Coriander took a deep breath and looked around the group at everyone's faces; Branch, Lillian, Sandburr, Carla, Radish… "I'm ready," she said.

One by one, heads nodded in agreement. Coriander reached out and clicked the power off switch on the master control for the habitats. Then she began shaking, and Branch reached out and enfolded her in a hug and said, "It's the right thing to do, we all know it. But we know it's hard too. Thank you, Coriander."

Coriander looked up and smiled through her tears, "I know. And it will be easy for them, easier than the hunger was. They'll just get cold and then they'll hibernate. They won't hurt at all."

Radish wiped her own eyes dry and then said, "And they won't be wasted either; the chickens will love them."

Branch grinned at them both and then said, "And we can all start working on our new projects. With everyone helping to suggest more options for new food flavors, textures, scents and appearances, Lillian, Jerome and Tate will be able to get new products developed really quickly. Lillian, I can't thank you and Jerome enough for everything you two have already done to make it possible."

"Speaking of Tate, has anyone broken the news to him yet?" Lillian asked.

"Jerome's going to talk to him," Branch said.

"Why Jerome? Wouldn't it come better from one of, well, one of you?" Lillian asked.

"There is no more 'you,'" Sandburr reminded her, "We're all one family now."

Carla's deep dimples appeared again and she wrapped her fingers within his.

Branch and Coriander exchanged a glance, and then Branch replied, "We think he'll take it best from Jerome. They seem to have hit it off, and Tate needs to hear it from someone who 'gets' him."

Jerome followed Tate down the path alongside the rows of herbs, and grinned at the sight of one of Tate's hands coming up to yank at the waistband of the well-worn dungarees, and then both tanned hands retucking the plaid shirt back in. Jerome had his answer – here at the earthold Tate's clothes were loose and baggy, and nothing glittered.

Tate paused where the path forked off in a couple of directions and said, "The public buildings; meeting hall, group homes, kitchen, laundry, shop, showers and so forth are off that way, and the cabins for families or people who do better with more privacy are off this way. The reports you were asking about are in my cabin – so we can stop off there, and then head back to the kitchen to help with the evening meal."

The cabin was only three rooms, a living room open to the kitchen, and off that, a bedroom and bathroom, but Tate saw that Jerome was looking around with pleasure. "It's nice – homey," Jerome said.

Tate smiled faintly, he should have guessed Jerome would appreciate it, in spite of its simplicity. Then he walked to the shelf to pull down a couple of binders and lay them on the table. "Did you want to look at these now, or take them with you to read later?" Tate asked.

"Maybe in a minute. So, 'Tate'?" Jerome tilted his head and eyed him from a quizzical angle. "I thought all of you Eartholders had names of plants or animals or something like that. How'd you end up with a citiname?"

"Tate is short for Tater," he replied shortly.

Jerome tilted his head in the other direction and looked even more mystified. A short laugh involuntarily pressed thru Tate's lips. It was refreshing to see Jerome's thoughts displayed so clearly in his expression. Tate was so weary of being surrounded by people constrained to hide every thought.

"Tate, Tater, Potater, Potato," Tate recited. "Tate is short for Potato – my given name."

"Ah, I get it now," Jerome said. His expression cleared and he smiled, "I like it. Potato has … substance. It's solid, sturdy. Nice name. Why'd you shorten it?"

The answering smile that had been forming on Tate's face vanished. He shrugged, his eyes distant.

"Hey – Tate!" Jerome said and waved a hand in front of his face, "Where'd you go? Did I ask a too-personal question?"

Tate pressed his lips together and then reluctantly offered up an explanation, "I never really felt I fitted in with everyone at the earthold as a kid, and I suppose I thought I would rather be a part of SNN. But then when I was at SNN, and saw for myself how unconnected everyone there is to the living world and how little most of them understand about diversity and the balance it provides – well, I guess I realized I hadn't valued what I had, what everyone has at the eartholds."

"You know," Jerome said, "I'm really glad you mentioned that – diversity. Because, well, you know my pitch to Seth?"

"Yes. 'To use the ecological richness preserved within the eartholds as a resource to research increased diversity in food products.' But you realize that your products at the café are what really convinced him?" Tate asked.

"Right," Jerome said, and then cast a sidelong look at Tate and added, "Well, I have a confession to make. Lillian and I have been working together, with other scientists and eartholds, to try to pursue this same kind of research, as a way to increase the economic importance of eartholds."

"And, well, I think that provides a really much better option in the long-term than your SeaSkater plan. Oh, for the short-term, if the eartholds could really step up and provide all the food needed, you might gain some support, but really if you think about it, there wouldn't be any diversification of power, you'd just be trading Seth's control over the world food supply, for your earthold's control of it. I know you think it would be controlled more ethically, and I don't disagree, but honestly, I think there's a real danger that any act of terrorism will make most people want to ensure the eartholds have less control, not more."

"Deep down, I think you must know that threatening the existing food supply isn't the best way to protect the eartholds. Can you... would you consider abandoning the SeaSkater project?"

Tate stared angrily at Jerome. He'd hoped they were on the same page, that they'd be able to work together. Had he misjudged him after all? "I've worked a long time on that project, and it hasn't always been easy," Tate said fiercely, "I don't really- "

"Tate," Jerome interrupted softly, "You must know Seth would find out you were behind it. And then what?"

"I don't care about that. He needs to be stopped," Tate said stubbornly.

"Tate," Jerome pursued gently, "If the eartholds can become economically important to the development of new food products, Seth won't have a monopoly over the world food supply any longer. Control would become diversified. Wouldn't you rather be alive to see that day, than pursue the SeaSkater project, and risk him realizing you used his own resources to try to destroy him?"

Tate stared at Jerome. He had it all figured out. Jerome somehow understood that deep down, for Tate it was just as much about destroying Seth, as it was about protecting the eartholds.

"C'mon, Tate, agree with me! Please?" Jerome asked.

Tate took in the entreaty in Jerome's eyes, and the tension in his shoulders.

"Just for argument sake," Tate said carefully, "Suppose I agreed to set aside the SeaSkater project – for awhile – how would you propose to make the eartholds economically important – and prevent Seth from controlling them as well?"

Jerome smiled, "We're already part of the way there, Tate! Lillian and I have been keeping it as quiet as possible, so that Seth wouldn't learn about it too soon, but there are already a couple of dozen different HighHundred families that have invested in new food product research. That's been in the works for a couple of years, and there are a little more than eighty food product 'recipes' that have been developed. No market testing of course – that would have gotten back to Seth in a heartbeat, but they're pretty much ready for production."

"Wait a minute!" Tate said, "If you've got all that backing, and you've got all those products ready – why the hell did you even approach Seth?"

"Because he's got the FDA and all the other regulatory agencies in his pocket. They've got the regulations written so tightly that it's almost impossible for anyone else to get a new product accepted for production. Now, if Seth requests that the nutrition guidelines for new food manufacturing are broadened – to make the road clear for his new product lines, he'll inadvertently clear the road for everyone else too. By the time he realizes what's happened, it will be too late; there will be dozens of products on the market faster than he can get his one or two or three new products out there. Especially since while he's been quietly reducing food scientist staff in the companies he owns or controls, Lillian and I and the others have been just as quietly hiring them," Jerome replied.

"That's… that's incredible," Tate said. He could barely take it in. It could mean, it could mean a different world. A world in which the eartholds were secure, and… for the first time in years, he allowed himself to consider a life after Seth. For long moments, while Jerome stayed quiet and let him, Tate thought about the work that must have been necessary – the work that Jerome and Lillian had accomplished.

"Jerome, I… I have to thank you. You and Lillian. I thought I was pretty much alone in this," Tate said quietly.

Jerome's eyes glinted with pleasure. It was such a relief. Tate could have been angry, angry at being undermined, at having his plans overset, and being 'upstaged' by someone else's work supplanting his own. But no, in spite of Seth's influence, at heart he was still an honorable man.

"So, Tate, you're okay with setting the SeaSkater project aside?" Jerome asked.

"I guess so," Tate said slowly. What would he do, now that he didn't have to devote his life to that project? Didn't have to keep in Seth's good graces?

"Good, because I have another confession," Jerome said.

Tate frowned as Jerome brought his hands in front of him and knotted them together nervously.

"What is it?" Tate asked.

"Last night, the others; Lillian, Sandburr, Coriander, Branch, Radish, Carla; they all voted, and I suppose there might have been others from your earthold who voted," Jerome said jerkily, "They all voted to terminate the SeaSkater project. And they deputized me to tell you," Jerome finished in a rush.

For a moment, Tate sat silent. And then he shook his head and laughed. "And here I was thinking how nice a change it is to talk with someone who just says the first thing that pops into his head," he said, "and instead... how long did you spend planning this conversation?"

Jerome looked sheepish and muttered, "Three hours."

"Three hours!" Tate exclaimed.

"Yeah, well, it was important to me to get this right," Jerome said seriously, "I... I respect you and I knew you must... must have good reasons for wanting to serve Seth up in some of his own sauce."

Tate narrowed his eyes, and then raised an eyebrow questioningly. "Yeah – and just how did you know that?" he asked.

"Lillian passed on your warning. It was... I couldn't believe how unselfish you were. You didn't even know me, and you were looking out for me. And in the restaurant..." Jerome paused and then resumed, "Tate... I... I'd like for us to continue to work together. I hope you'll forgive me for not being completely honest. I wanted to tell you everything at the restaurant, but it was Lillian and the others' secret too – and I couldn't share it until they agreed."

"You want me to work on the products for Seth's new food line?" Tate asked.

"Well, it might actually be safer if you passed that on to someone else, just so you wouldn't fall under suspicion by Seth later. But maybe we could work on some other project?" Jerome asked.

"Like what, Jerome? I'm not a scientist, you know," Tate said sourly. He'd been looking forward to partnering with Jerome on that project.

Jerome looked sympathetic, "You've got a scientist's mind, it's a pity you didn't have more opportunity to pursue it earlier, but hey, nothing's stopping you now from doing whatever you like, whatever you find exciting. And I'd help. Just tell me what…" Jerome stopped and then slowly a smile spread over his face, and he looked at Tate mischievously.

"Tate," Jerome said with a voice now slightly lowered in timbre, "What do you find… exciting? Whatever it is, I'd like to help; help you make it happen." Jerome's eyes were bright, and intent on his.

Tate looked at Jerome with suddenly widened eyes. His breath held suspended in his chest. What was Jerome suggesting? Tate had felt a few times before that there might be something like attraction working between them. Was he seeing, feeling, an invitation? If so…

Tate took a step closer to Jerome and looked into those dark eyes that now seemed so welcoming. "I think," Tate began and then took a little breath and began again, "I think that now, now I might find it exciting to… start over." Was it enough of a hint, should he have said start over with someone new? Lillian never had said whether or not Jerome…

Jerome's smile softened to something deeper, more serious, and then he reached out to take Tate's hand in his. His eyes soft on Tate's, he said quietly, "You know, I've been thinking for quite a while that there is a kind of connection working between us." He tilted his head slightly and asked, "What do you think? It's not only the similar goals, is it? It's more the intangible - the way we just... like each other?"

Tate stood unmoving for several seconds. Was it really going to be that easy? That simple? Finally he looked into Jerome's steady eyes, let his hand return the firm grasp, and managed to say, "Yeh – yes."

Jerome's eyes lit in a grin, and an answering smile formed on Tate's face. He hadn't dreamed of this. Hadn't dared to dream of it - but Jerome's arms wrapped around him now in a hug filled with affection and exuberance.

"Jerome, you... you know we'll need to be careful; it won't do for Seth to think I've chosen you over him."

"But you have, right?" Jerome grinned.

Tate grinned back and said, "Yeah, but we'll have to plan this out, figure a way to-"

"Later," Jerome said, and leaned in for a kiss.

DOMO
By Debbie Painter

She was a skinny, rickety-looking little thing full of angles and taut flesh. Her mass of dark hair had never completely succumbed to a proper haircut during her time with them, and people swore that all that blackness disguised two pointed ears. Everyone in the village knew that her incisor teeth were pointed and sharp like an animal's. Anyone could see them, after all. Those strange teeth were no secret, and Domo made no effort to hide them.

At first, her odd appearance made some of the village folks nervous for fear that she was a devil or something possessed by demons. "My grandmother told me the tale," old Yakob said, "of sky beings who fell to the earth and lived amongst men. They were wicked, terrible beings who ate children."

"You old fool," Mioma countered, "she is a child. She is not going to eat herself." Mioma did not tolerate fools, and she especially did not tolerate old Yakob. They argued day after day when he came to her soup stall in the market to eat, and all the village laughed at their on-going feud. Yet sometimes she looked at the child's differences and wondered.

No one had seen such a being as Yakob told of, of course, but many of them, especially the old folk, told the tales that had been passed down to them. There were many stories of the sky beings who were sometimes protectors and sometimes the enemy, but this girl was unlike any of those descriptions. For days the village was abuzz with the news of the foundling, but slowly with the passage of time the rumors ended and the girl had simply become Domo, the village mute.

The people of the village called her Domo because they did not know her name. She did not smile nor did she speak.

The villagers had not thought so much about it when she arrived, thinking she was only a frightened child scared speechless by her experience, but as time passed they realized she would not or could not. Such a strange little girl. Of course, she was not one of them, and who knew what kind of people lived beyond the horizon? Perhaps, everyone where Domo came from was mute and strange. Who could tell? The villagers themselves had not traveled far, and often three or four seasons passed without a visit from someone beyond this place.

One day she had simply arrived stumbling across the vast, empty plain, filthy, starving, and covered with ash and dirt. The little village consisted only of twenty or so families living in their small mud brick residences, tidy outbuildings for the beasts, and all the residences built around a central square. It was obvious that this little girl did not belong to anyone here for everyone knew everyone else. Men from the village had followed the dirt path they thought she had taken eastward for half a day or so without finding anyone or any sign of her people and had hurried home at dark without a clue to the identity of the silent, strange little girl who had wandered into their midst. Womenfolk had clucked over her as women tend to do when a child is involved, and they had found her food and clothing, bathed her tiny body, and tended her little hurts. From what they saw, it appeared she had been alone for days, and they wondered how so young a child could have been lost.

There was only one home in the village without children. Mioma lived alone in her small hut and had been without a mate since her husband had died seasons earlier. With so many already having too many children, it was easy to determine who should be asked to take in the new girl. Mioma took her in in place of the husband and child she had lost, and those with many children offered her what they could afford to give away for the little foundling. For a while, Domo was the center of concern in the town, but after a while people forgot the mystery that was Domo.

"You were the scrawniest little thing," Mioma would tell Domo later. "When I saw you, I thought of a little bird early out of its nest. Those big black eyes and all that black hair! I knew that you would be perfect for me."

In time, Domo grew and became strong among them. Her flesh rounded, her hair grew shiny, and her eyes brightened. It soon became evident that despite her lack of speech she was alert and intelligent. Each day she and Mioma were at the marketplace selling their soup and fritters to the day laborers. It was their only source of income, and they made a small living at it, enough to replace what they had cooked and buy more vegetables to make their soup. There was rarely any extra for sweets or little things that girls sometimes wanted. If Domo had any such desires, no one knew because in that she was as silent as she was in all things. Domo cooked and she cleaned and she sold soup in the market. That was the beginning and the end of her life or so they thought.

"Domo," Mioma would say, "she is a good girl. Do what I say. No disobedience. Strange girl but no trouble."

Domo, of course, said nothing.

For seasons after her arrival, the village went on as it had for generation upon generation. New buildings were erected around the town square as the young people grew up and started their own families. The people lived close to the land and its rhythm was their life. Trees were planted in the village and grew tall, providing shade in the summer and breaks from the wind in the winter. In the spring, fields were plowed and crops planted in the loamy, brown fields and the freehorns were shorn for their abundant wool. The earth was fertile and so rich it took little effort from the farmers other than keeping the weeds from the crop and ensuring there was sufficient water. While the men tilled the green and ample fields, the women spun the wool, made fabric, and prepared simple garments for themselves and their kin. When the harvest came, everyone worked the fields and orchards whether they had a field or orchard to work or not. It was not their way for one to put himself over another. Each member of the village invested somehow in the food that was raised, and in turn each person received a portion of the benefits. Mioma and Domo ate then with rare abundance but were careful to dry and preserve a portion of their produce for the soup that would help keep them fed through the next winter and spring.

Domo's eyes would sparkle in those times, and it made old Mioma laugh. "I know that you are getting enough to eat," she would tease. "Where will you put all that extra food?" Domo would give her a rare smile, something guaranteed to assure that an extra portion would appear on her plate during that time of bounty. Mioma's only regret then was the child's continued silence which separated her from Mioma and the other villagers and always made her an outsider.

After the harvest, life in the village moved from the fields and lanes to the simple, tidy homes of its occupants. Winter was a quiet time when the men could repair their farm implements, make harnesses or other tack for the beasts of burden, and take an occasional cup of ale in the tavern. The long, dark evenings were no burden. It gave them more time to sleep. And if someone had asked about how they were entertained during this time, they would only have received curious looks. Freedom from labor was a pleasant, anticipated gift of winter and had no other value than the relaxation it offered. They simply lived, and they lived simply.

The only things that really changed from season to season were the babies who were born, the children who grew to adulthood, and the old who died. It was a fact of their lives as it was in all other beings that things changed and that life was not permanent. While the dead were still mourned, it was understood that this was all in the nature of things and that grief was in the parting. It was simply the way things were, and the flow of life and death was never challenged.

Domo, too, was growing toward adulthood. Mioma noticed that Domo's legs were beginning to lengthen, her little nipples darken, and hair grow in places where it previously had not. Mioma had caught Domo a couple of times looking at the village boys, and she knew that the girl's heart was beginning to open as girls' hearts did in their time. She needed, Mioma knew, to talk with the girl about being a woman.

"Domo," the old woman began one night as they sat around the warm, bright fire, the wind howling outside, "it is time that we speak of changes that are to come to you."

The girl's gaze turned to her, her black eyes and long black hair shining in the firelight. It could just be, Mioma realized, that this scrawny little girl is going to make a beauty. Such a thing had never occurred to Mioma before, and that made her task even more important. Domo's body was beginning to change. Her dark hair was thick and attractive, her eyes luminous, and her lips the palest of pinks. Even growing up in a small village where everyone was likely to be some degree of kin, Mioma knew what happened to pretty girls if they were not careful and smart.

"I don't know the ways of your people, Domo," Mioma continued. "I can only tell you what I know of mine. There are some differences between us and we may not be made exactly the same. But when you become a woman your body will change and you will be prepared to make children. Do you understand?"

Domo's face was very still as she considered what she had heard. Such a thoughtful girl. Then she smiled and touched the top of her head, showing it extending above her. Good, Mioma thought; Domo knew she would grow taller. The child giggled softly and touched her belly, showing an imaginary bubble extending from it. Very well. She understood that a woman's place in life was to bear children.

"Right," Mioma cooed. "You will grow taller and wider, and your body will change even more. If your body is like mine, there will be a day when you are ready to grow a baby in your belly. When you do not grow a baby, the body casts off that preparation for another moon until it is ready to try again. You will bleed and it is normal for females."

The child's frightened expression told it all. She had not known this.

"Do not worry, child. It is normal. It will not hurt." The rapport she had desired established, Mioma went on to tell Domo about her life as a woman. They spent the time from the waning of the sun until the rising of the moon in this discussion, using words and gestures. When Mioma finished, Domo touched her hand gently and smiled. Mioma took it as a sign of her thanks.

Mioma's preparations had been wise, it happened. Domo began to flower as a young woman in the spring, and that was about the time that things in the village began to change.

The springtime was when people began to come out of their houses in the late light and sit together in their doorways watching the approach of darkness. Flowers bloomed in well-tended gardens, and the silver birds settled in to sing softly before they roosted for the night in the tall trees. Domo had a particular fondness for listening to the neighbors talk, Mioma knew, and tried to allow it whenever possible. Girls needed to know the ways of women, after all. It was a time for gossip between the women or exchange of recipes. The men primarily sat with their pipes, relaxing after a long day's work.

One night as they sat in the doorway waiting for darkness to fall, strange lights appeared in the sky. Domo pointed excitedly to some specks of light in the eastern sky where it was darkest. Moving stars? Curious. They danced and moved for hours. Those things made Domo very excited, and Mioma wondered what significance the girl found in the dancing lights. Mioma herself had never seen such lights before, but certainly as distant as they were those points of light had no bearing on themselves. Yet she could and did take pleasure in the child's delight at those bright and pretty things so far away.

"What do you think they are?" she asked curiously.

Domo frowned, lacking the words she needed to explain.

"What does it remind you of, child?" the older woman

pressed. "Have you seen something like it before?"

But the girl had no words or gestures for what she felt, and Mioma ended her questioning, trying to spare the child. There was no point in asking questions that could not be answered.

The next morning there were strange clouds on the distant horizon. They were of a color no one could remember seeing before and lightning danced in them. Also, they were not exactly like the storm clouds the villagers had seen before, but were strange colors and shapes.

"Have you ever seen such clouds?" they asked one another.

"I remember in the year of the great snows," old Yakob swore, "that there were green clouds in the skies."

Mioma laughed. "Yakob," she hooted, "if there is anything to be said, you will say it whether it is right or not."

Domo smiled at Mioma's joke, something she rarely did.

Mioma watched Domo watch the clouds. Something seemed to have suddenly come alive in the child, and her eyes gleamed as she watched the lightning dance in the luminescent haze so far away that they could not even hear the sound of its thunder. The child was entranced and Mioma was glad that the girl had finally found something that touched her imagination.

Occasionally, Domo gestured and tried to make hand talk along with the others, and the village folk all encouraged her to join them in the full expression of their lives. But no one really understood what Domo struggled to reveal.

Each day the clouds seemed taller and closer. After three or four days, no one really noticed them anymore except for Domo who followed their progress expectantly. Mioma, who was watching Domo, did not know what would happen. In the seasons the child had lived with her, Mioma had never seen the girl like this; eyes so bright and expectant, excitement visible. Yes, Domo was different.

"Domo!" old Yakob yelled the next day. "You must pay attention. You have spilled my soup all over me, foolish, wasteful girl!"

Mioma whirled. Sure enough, the old man was telling the truth for once. His soup was all over his tunic and the ground. Frustrated, she cuffed the girl across the ear, causing her to cry out with surprise. Mioma had never touched Domo in anger before, and her angry outburst was a surprise to them both. Domo's face intensified. She hadn't liked being struck. For a moment, the air seemed to thicken and warm around them. Then, just as abruptly, all was well again.

"I'm sorry, Domo," Mioma said after a moment. "I should not have hit you, but you also should not have spilled Yakob's soup. You know that we do not eat if we do not sell soup."

The girl nodded that she understood and poured the old man a second bowl, placing it carefully before him. Then she turned to her caretaker, made sure that they were at peace, and went back to her work. Still Mioma noticed that Domo regarded her differently when she would catch her eye.

The clouds disappeared or, perhaps, the clouds overtook them. A strange, hot breeze began that afternoon that was filled with dust and unusual smells. It stained the tan brick buildings a soft red. The air began to smell different as well. It reminded Mioma of the smithy forge when it was very hot and Walla the smith was at his busiest. Here and there, people sneezed and coughed from the dust, but it did not alarm them. Spring had been drier than usual, and it was only a little dust storm, they said. But Mioma noticed that the child appeared to be upset and anxious now.

In the morning, they found the chickens dead, but with no marks on any of them. Every chicken in the village was dead. It was a catastrophe. The men met to decide what was to be done, but no one had a suggestion. This was simply beyond their collective experience. Even old Yakob, who claimed to know everything, was silent. In the end, there was no choice. A pit was dug on the edge of the village, and every dead chicken was burned to prevent this thing from going further.

As night approached, unease settled over the village. Domo came to Mioma and took her hand, trying to lead her from their little house.

"What are you doing, child?" Mioma chided. "It will be dark soon, and there is no moon tonight. It will be truly dark."

Domo persisted, her eyes large. She pulled at Mioma again, trying to get her to leave.

The old woman patted the child's face gently. "Domo," she said gently, "we are all upset by what has happened, but do not be frightened. One of the men will walk over to Rappi and buy some chickens. We will have chicks again soon."

Domo only shook her head in negation and said nothing.

The next morning the freehorns were all dead; every single one, and still not a visible injury on any of them. The men did not bother to meet this time. They simply dug another pit and burned the sheep as well. The black, thick smoke reeked of burned wool and flesh.

"This village is cursed," Yakob said to anyone who would listen.

Walla the smith swore as he dismissed the old man, "We have had bad times before. There will be bad times again, maybe this spring. But this is our place and these are our lives. What else is there for us to do?"

"Domo tried to get me to leave last night," Mioma mentioned in passing. "She was very frightened, poor little thing. There is no telling what has happened to her before that would make her so afraid like that."

"Yes," Yebba the weaver remembered, "she looked like she had had a bad time when she came to us. So hungry and dirty. Maybe the animals dying reminds her of what happened to her before, Mioma."

"For all the good it will do any of us," Yakob fumed. "If she knew what was wrong, Domo could not tell us."

Domo worked in the soup stall as Mioma did, hearing what the villagers were saying about her. She did her job as faithfully as always. And she watched the sky.

The wails of Walla's wife Boku woke the village the next morning as she screamed over the body of her newborn baby. Walla and Boku had tried for many years to have a baby, and they had finally succeeded just two moons earlier. But now the baby, like the sheep and the chickens, was dead.

The women of the village gathered around Boku to bathe the baby, wrap its little body in a shroud, and convey it to the grave the men had dug.

As they left the cemetery, Domo took Mioma's hand and again tried to lead her from the village.

"Child, what is it? What do you want?" Mioma asked with frustration. "Can't you see that this is no time for your foolishness?"

In frustration, the girl brushed her bushy hair back off her forehead. She slapped herself with frustration once and had started to do it again when Mioma took her hand, stilling it.

"Domo, what do you want to say?"

The girl looked into her caretaker's eyes, her anger and resentment evident. Here was a good mind that lacked expression, a good heart that cried out to her surrogate mother to beware, and she had no means of sharing that inner life with anyone.

"Domo, why should we leave the village?"

A group of adults had gathered around them, and Domo found herself the center of attention. She looked around then picked up a stick with a sharp point and drew in the sand. First, she drew stars. Stars that looked like suns. Stars that looked like moons. Others that were shaped unlike anything the village people had ever seen. When she finished and knew she had everyone's attention, she looked around the circle and pointed to herself.

"We know you like stars, sweetheart," Mioma said. "Why did you draw them?"

Domo patted herself then pointed to the stars.

"I think she means that she sees the stars," another woman said.

Domo shook her head in negation. Picking up a small

stone, she patted her drawing and then pointed to the stone which she dropped to the ground.

"Surely she is not saying that she came from the stars," another said. "That is impossible. That exists only in old wives' tales."

But Domo jumped in delighted acknowledgment of just that. She repeated the gesture again.

"You came from the stars?" Mioma asked.

Domo threw herself at Mioma's neck nodding frantically as she hugged her.

"Why did you not tell us before?"

Domo nodded negatively. That was too complicated a question for her to answer in this fashion. She smoothed out the sand and began to draw boxes. Within minutes, a representation of a village or a town appeared. Then she pointed at herself and the town.

"You came from this village?" Mioma asked.

Bigger, Domo gestured. Much bigger.

"You came from a city?"

Domo hugged her in delighted acknowledgment.

"Why did you leave?"

For a moment, Domo's face darkened before she began to gather small stones from the surrounding sand. That task accomplished, she began to throw the stones one by one into the image of her hometown. Within moments, the city disappeared.

"There was a war? Or the town was destroyed?"

Domo nodded.

"How did you come to be here? Where are your people?"

Sadness filled the dark eyes. She pantomimed walking along and then fell to the ground. She did not move.

"They died?"

Domo opened her eyes and nodded solemnly.

"Why are you here?"

Domo smiled. She took Mioma's hand and began to lead her from the village.

"You are here to lead us?"

Finally understood, Domo smiled broadly.

"Why should we believe such a wild, extravagant claim?" Beera the butcher asked. "She can tell us anything, but she has absolutely nothing to back her up."

"Why should we leave here?" Mioma asked, trying to believe in the child.

Domo gestured again. One, two, three nights ago, she signaled, there were stars in the sky. The war people have come back, and we must flee, she seemed to say.

"I, for one, am not going anywhere," Beera insisted. "My family has lived here for generations, and nothing like that has ever happened. Why should I believe a half-wit child who can't even talk?"

Mioma turned on him. "Don't you say that about her, Beera! Sure, Domo can't speak, but she is plenty smart."

"You can go wherever you want. I am not going anywhere," he insisted.

"Then don't go," Mioma said. "Stay here. I'm not sure I'm convinced either, but I'm not going to close my mind off to the notion. I'm going to talk with Domo some more tonight. You may join us if you wish."

Mioma had hoped many would come to their small home to join in her discussion with her child that evening, but none did. It was growing dark and the others went to their beds as though nothing had happened. So the two of them sat before the fire alone in the chill spring evening air and talked as best they could using Mioma's words and Domo's gestures.

"You do know something about what is happening, don't you, Domo?" Mioma asked as they settled in for the evening. The girl nodded in affirmation. "And you believe that it is dangerous for us to stay here?" Again, the child signaled agreement.

"Domo, how do you know this? You were so young when you came to us. How can you remember your time elsewhere? Why are you so sure?'

The girl shrugged noncommittally and then took one of Mioma's hands placing it over her own heart.

"Your heart tells you so?"

Mioma was silent for long moments. With Domo's lack of speech, it had often been so between them, and they were comfortable in the quiet. Outside, they heard the voices of men on their way home for the evening from the tavern and the distant bark of dogs. All together, it was an unremarkable evening...except that they needed to take their own futures into their hands.

The prospect of leaving everything she knew was a daunting one for Mioma. She had never been outside the village before, and she knew no one in this other world to which she was considering traveling. Would there be someone to help them if the need arose? Could they make their way somewhere else without the need of cooking and selling soup every day? Was it possible for her to walk away from everyone and everything she had ever known simply on the belief of this child, this mute girl?

Yet there was something compelling in the notion. To give up this lonely life and search out another one, to make a place somewhere where there was abundance, not just survival, for everyone. Yes, those were both desirable goals, but was that enough in the end?

Mioma looked around the hovel that she had called home since she married Bartook. Oh, he had been such a strong, sweet-natured boy when they married. Bartook was a gentle giant; tall, muscular like a bull, and as easy to lead as a lamb. They had been so much in love, and Mioma flushed with pleasure once more when she thought of those times. For seasons, they had been happy together. Their only regret was that children had not come, and when one did, tiny Anka, the baby was frail, small, and sickly. She lived for two seasons before they had to return her to the soil once more. There were no more children after that.

Domo had been such a blessing to her after Bartook's death. Few single men remained in the village because there were few unattached women. After Bartook died, there were no available men for many seasons, and eventually Mioma had relinquished the dream of another husband as she had let go so many other dreams.

Mioma refocused, thinking of the girl. "Do you really think we should leave?" she asked carefully.

Domo's head nodded emphatically.

Mioma looked around their small lodging. This had been her home with her husband, the only place her baby had ever lived, and it was all she had ever had, but wasn't Domo her future now? Didn't Domo's peace of mind and her safety count for something? Again, Mioma looked around the small hut. They would need food, water and something to keep them protected from the elements. What they needed to take, they could carry on their backs.

"I believe you," Mioma said. "We will prepare in the morning."

Disbelief greeted Mioma the next morning when she prepared to take leave of the village.

"A grown woman like you is going to just walk away from everything she has ever known?" one woman said.

"How can you follow that half-wit girl?" asked another.

"Domo has as much sense as anyone here," Mioma said defensively. "We don't know what happened to her before she came here, but she may remember something that is important from her before time."

"'May remember'," the woman scoffed. "That is a lot to change your life on, Mioma."

"Nonetheless, we are going. You may come if you wish."

"I'm not going anywhere, and if you do, Mioma, you are a fool."

They packed their few possessions, a few pots, their preserved food, their few clothes, and the bedding they slept on. "If we do not return," Mioma said, "someone may take this place. Leave it empty for a few seasons and we shall see."

Then she took her daughter's hand, back straight and proud, and walked west away from the village into the flat, open plain. It occurred to Mioma as they went that Domo had arrived from the east and was leaving to the west. That arrangement seemed curiously symmetrical to her.

The second midday after their departure, Mioma had begun to think of how they might take another meal. Since their departure in the early morning light, she had only seen a single water source, and that spring was far behind them. Looking for water so that they might save what they carried, Mioma began to plan. Then the earth dipped under their feet, a flash blinded them, and within moments they heard a tremendous roar. Whirling, they both saw a large cloud back along the trajectory over which they had traveled. The village was in an almost straight line behind them and the cloud.

Domo looked at the scene in frantic disbelief. She took Mioma's hand and pulled forward desperately.

"What? What is it? What does this mean?" Mioma asked.

Fearfully, Domo pulled her hand, her head shaking. There was clearly not time for discussion anymore, Mioma realized. Whatever was occurring was as close as the village and less than two days' walk away. Although she did not know what she was fleeing, Mioma yielded to the frantic pressure of her child's hand and picked up the pace of their walking. Afraid, she looked about them trying to think of some way that they might seek cover, but the broad plain was as flat as the table where her customers had eaten her soup and there was no means of concealment as far as her eyes could see.

There was no midday meal. Domo's fear propelled them forward at the quickest speed their legs could manage. Barely stopping to relieve themselves, the two females trotted across the featureless landscape. In the late afternoon, Mioma could see something appear on the distant horizon. When she first noticed it, she was uncertain what she was seeing, but as they continued their hurried walk she realized that a range of low-lying hills was rising before them. That promised refuge and protection from the unknown terror that followed in their wake.

Breathlessly, Mioma pointed and Domo took her hand smiling. If they could reach those hills before the thing behind them caught up with them, they had a chance to hide and be safe. But even as Mioma had those thoughts she wondered what they had seen that morning. That cloud seemed so much larger than the other ones which they had seen days before. Of course, she reasoned, it would look larger if it was much, much closer.

Once they stopped to catch their wind and to look behind them. Heat mirages danced blackly across the scene making features appear where there were none. There was no cloud now, no pall of dust, no flashing lightning as there had been when they saw strange occurrences in the sky before. But Domo was as determined as ever to move forward and grasped Mioma's hand, moving her ever onward. Despite the unknown ahead, Domo was still frightened of the unknown behind.

"I need to eat and get some water," Mioma said, uncertain that she could keep up this pace without becoming ill.

Domo stopped for a moment as though debating and then nodded her head in agreement.

They had a small meal and some of their precious water and rested for a short while. It was good, Mioma reflected, to simply sit for a while on the brown earth and let the warmth of the spring sunshine warm her tired body. Since leaving the village, they had not spent any time resting other than when they had slept at night, and she was feeling it.

"Do we have to go on?" she questioned, knowing that the answer would not be what she wanted.

Domo smiled sadly and nodded. The girl put away their food while her caretaker sat, and when she was ready to move on she offered Mioma a hand so that she could rise. As the sun began to set, they plodded along the same path on which they had left the village the day before, looking over their shoulders from time to time to mark whether they were being pursued.

When it became too dark for them to see the path anymore, Mioma and Domo stopped for the night, lying down to an impromptu camp without a campfire. "We don't want the draw any attention, do we?" she had reasoned with the girl, and Domo seemed to agree. Lying on the ground without the benefit of any light source made them both uneasy, and their sleep was fragmented. Once, Mioma heard Domo cry out as though she was having a nightmare, but when she touched the girl Domo subsided into quiet sleep.

At first light, they were moving again. The encroaching darkness the previous evening had concealed the approach of the low hills, and with new light they could see that destination should be within their reach today.

"What do you think is there?" Mioma asked. "Is this a good place for us?"

Domo smiled and patted her hand softly.

"Will we be safe?"

The smile faltered. Then Domo nodded slowly. Yes, she indicated, they would be secure within those beckoning hills, but Mioma questioned her truthfulness for the first time.

Just after midday, they crossed the first stream. It was a beautiful little thing that gurgled and sang through a small valley as the water bounced from stone to stone on its way elsewhere. The two took their midday meal at the side of the creek, sitting on the moss-covered stones. The cool, moist air was a relief after their long walk, and Mioma began to feel she could finally relax.

But she was wrong. When they picked up the trail once more, the path they had been taking simply seemed to disappear. Confused, Mioma and Domo searched to find their way and lost hours of travelling time before they concluded that they were hopelessly lost. The sun was beginning to dip into the distant horizon.

"I thought you knew where you were going," Mioma remarked sharply. "How could you have let us get lost? You wanted to come out here, not me, and now you have lost us."

But then Mioma thought, 'What am I doing?' She started over again. "I'm sorry. I shouldn't have said that. I am frightened and uncertain." She pulled the girl to her and hugged her gently. "I am the adult and this is my fault, not yours. I have brought you out here and now we are lost."

Domo shook her head in denial. Pulling away from Mioma's grasp, she sat down on a nearby rock and patted one adjoining it, indicating that her caretaker should join her. Domo pulled out another package of food and divided it between the two of them. Clearly, she was prepared to wait.

"Domo," Mioma finally asked, "what are we running from?"

The girl's eyes widened at the question. After a moment of reflection, she shrugged helplessly. The older woman was uncertain whether that meant that Domo did not know or whether she lacked the words to answer the question. It was often so frustrating, Mioma reflected, to know that such a good mind could not express what was within it.

"Do you know?"

Domo nodded in affirmation. She knew what they faced, even if she could not say it, and Mioma worried what was locked within that mind.

"Are we in danger, Domo?"

Suddenly, the girl looked very young and terribly sad. It was clear to Mioma that she did not want to answer.

"So we are in danger." This time it was not a question.

The girl nodded in agreement. Then, rising, she cleared an area in the soft, nearby soil, found a short stick, and began to draw. From the hands of the child flowed wondrous pictures; stars, clouds, strange vessels in the sky. Mioma was captivated by the images before her. She had never seen anything like it.

"How did you learn to draw so quickly?" she asked. "A few days ago, you did not have such skill."

Domo only smiled sweetly and put her finger over her mouth. A secret, of course, like so much of the girl's life seemed to be.

"What is following us?"

Abruptly, the girl's eyes fell, and her entire demeanor changed. Rubbing away the first image, she drew another one, horrific and frightening. It spoke of explosions and fire and destruction. When she looked at Mioma again, there were tears in her eyes.

"What is that?"

Domo shrugged, her mood desolate. Mioma pulled the girl to her and hugged her gently. "Whatever may come, my girl," she said, "we will be together."

Domo wilted into her arms, seeming tired of being strong for once, and allowed her caretaker to comfort her. As they sat there waiting, the darkness finally fell. As it grew, the stars began to fall from the distant sky.

The sun rose to reveal an appalling sight. Arrayed before them on the vast plain were creatures; things that Mioma had never seen, so strange that she even lacked the words to describe their horror. Hundreds, possibly thousands, and they were coming.

"What are they? What shall we do?" Mioma cried.

Domo set her shoulders and took a deep breath. She bent over, spit into the dirt, and made a paste from the mud. Then she picked it up and gestured toward Mioma's ears indicating that she needed to be able to touch them. Mioma held still until she felt the child putting the mud into her left ear and she jumped with surprise.

"What on earth are you doing?" she asked in amazement.

Domo gently pushed down the woman's upraised hands, showed her the mud again, and reached for her ear. Confused, Mioma subsided and allowed the child to cover one ear and then the other with the muddy paste. Domo smiled at her and when she finished she moved forward to give her caretaker a gentle kiss.

"What is that for?" Mioma asked.

Domo simply took her hand and placed it over her heart. Again her lack of words weighed on Mioma, and she decided that this must mean Domo was pleased at her compliance. Then the girl pushed her down behind a rocky shelf, indicated she should stay there, and started to move away.

"Wait! Where are you going? What are you doing?"

Domo pushed her down again, shook an angry finger at her, and turned to meet the oncoming army. As she walked away, Mioma lay in the dust confused and uncertain. What was Domo planning? She tried to trust that Domo knew what she was doing, but it was difficult. There was so much unsaid between them, that trust was not always easy. But, her mind countered raggedly, Domo had known enough to get them this far, and hopefully she knew what she was doing, even if Mioma's heart quaked at the thought of the girl going out to meet the approaching beasts.

Climbing to a rocky point above the flat plain, Domo watched the approaching madness with a calm that surprised Mioma. The girl stood there for long moments, and the noise below them heightened as though her appearance had caused some change in the beings there. Their approach seemed to quicken until she put up her hands and began to speak.

"You do not belong here," Domo said, her voice loud enough to carry across the plain and melodic like bird song. "Leave and there will be no further problem."

Domo could talk? Why had she never spoken before? And what was she doing? She seemed to be provoking the advancing beasts. Mioma heard the chittering of the beings below build to a roar. She hazarded a look at them, realized that they seemed to be rushing forward now, and ducked back into her hiding place. Surely, they were lost.

"This is my last warning." Domo was tall and straight and proud as the lone girl faced the advancing menace who did not falter at her warning.

"So be it." Domo began to glow with a strange radiance and seemed to grow larger where she stood on the rocky ledge. Suddenly it seemed she was big, bigger, and bigger still. From a girl she changed into a fearsome creature, fierce and wild. Her black hair stood out from her head like flames, and her black eyes were bright as the sun. She put her head back, opened her mouth widely, and began to roar.

At least, Mioma concluded, that must be what she was hearing. The blast of sound must have been horrible, but the mud in her ears seemed to protect her from a sound that must otherwise be deafening. The rocks under her feet shrieked with the noise, small avalanches of stones skittered down the slopes, and small stones vibrated and exploded around her. Domo's roar went on and on, and just when Mioma began to think that she would lose her reason it ended. The silence, by contrast, rang like a bell in her ears.

Shakily, Mioma pushed herself to her feet to view what had happened. Finding Domo collapsed where she had stood, she rushed to the child's side to check on her. The girl was the Domo she knew once more, the same size as before, her black hair and eyes as they had always been. It was only as she examined her precious child that Mioma realized what had happened. Stunned, she turned to gawk in stupefaction at the scene. As far as she could see, the metal beasts lay broken and shattered. There was no movement anywhere that she could see, and the advance of those beings had ended. She did not understand.

"Domo, Domo, my dear," she cried as she tried to elicit a response from the motionless child. "What does this mean? What have you done? What kind of being are you that you could do this?"

"Do not grieve," the girl replied weakly. "I was born for this."

"I don't understand any of this. Why are these beasts here? And, my dear child, why did you never speak to me before?"

Domo raised a weak hand to stroke Mioma's hair. "There are many races who have mastered travel between the stars. It is a skill learned long ago, and it has been both a blessing and a curse. Many that my people met in their journeys were kind and welcoming peoples, but there were also many who cared little for others, taking only for their own. The Krepts destroyed my homeworld when I was a baby. We had warred with them periodically for centuries, and I was born to protect the homeworld and other worlds my people found worthy. But I was too young, untrained and weak to destroy them. They arrived at the wrong time for my talents to be used. My parents fled with the remnants of our people in our ships. We almost got away, but they caught us here and engaged our small armada over this planet."

"You mean you came from some other place? How is that possible?"

"These ways are not so strange. Many have the knowledge. Your people have been guarded and kept innocent of these abilities. Your world is very special, Mioma. It is exceptionally rich so the people here have been protected from the other worlds for centuries. You live simply, but it is a good life. My people found you worthy of our protection. But the Krepts coveted your world and sought to take it as their own, even before the fall of our people. We have battled here before as your legends tell. My family sent me here in the hopes that I would have a chance to grow old enough and wise enough to be your protector when the time came."

"Why didn't you speak?"

"My line has certain abilities that we have been able to enhance with the engineering of our bodies. My gift is what we call the 'loud speak'. My first words had to be the words for the protection of a world. They were the strongest words I would ever utter. If I used those words in everyday conversation, my power would be diminished, so I saved them for today."

"So you stayed mute all these years to save your power for the time it would be needed?"

"Yes. You and the people of our village have been kind to me. I don't know that my own parents could have been better, so it was easy for me to close my mouth when I remembered what I could do for you in your time of need."

"My blessed, blessed child. All those times that I wished you could speak, and you were remaining silent to protect us. What can I say?" Mioma stroked the black, shiny hair affectionately.

"Only say that you understand."

"I don't really, but I thank you. These weapons that were brought to our world would have killed us all. We had no defense against such beings. You took care of us all."

"Yes. At first when I arrived in the village, I was so young and afraid, but you made me feel safe and cared for, Mioma. After a while, I wanted to protect you and the villagers in return."

"You did." Mioma looked out across the littered plain uncertainly. "But what about all of this? There is so much death. The village is certainly lost. How will this place ever be the same again?"

"That is the surprise." Domo rose slowly and took Mioma's hand. "Come. We need to find shelter for this next part."

"Shelter? What do we need to take shelter from?"

Domo smiled. "You trusted me enough to leave the village. Please believe in me one more time."

Mioma rose and followed the firm grasp of the child's hand. Within a little while, they found a small cave and settled into it after they had collected more freehorn patties to burn. They were both exhausted and despite the early hour they slept.

When they woke again in the afternoon, there was a light rain falling which quickly became more intense. Soon they could not see outside the cave, and Mioma was glad that they had taken refuge there. But how did Domo know it was going to rain? There had hardly been a cloud in the sky when they sought the cover of the cave.

Their small fire warded off the chill of the intense rain, and the cave kept them from getting very wet. They had a meal and sat quietly watching the rain pour down. It continued most of the day, and when they grew tired they slept again.

The next morning broke chill and foggy. Another light meal warmed them, and afterward Domo moved to the rocky ledge outside the cave to view the indistinct landscape. Along the plain below, there was a thick layer of fog, but here and there a wisp of it floated toward the sky.

"Mioma, come here please," she asked.

When Mioma joined her, she could hardly believe her

eyes. The metal skeletons of the war machines and the bodies of the dead had almost disappeared overnight. As the fog lifted, she could see new growth on the plain before. At first she thought it was grass, but she quickly realized that she was wrong. Colors sprang to life that she had never seen. Plants seemed to grow almost before her eyes, and as the view cleared Mioma realized that they were growing from the wreckage of the destroyed army. The plain below was filling with plants and trees, even as she watched, and it was even more beautiful than this place had been before. She did not understand how that was possible, but Domo had created many wonders. Now she created life from death.

"It's all so beautiful," she murmured.

"Their bodies are becoming one with this good, healing world. They will trouble you no more because the goodness of this world is stronger than the evil of the Krept. It is for you, Mioma, because you believed in me, because you protected me, and because you loved me." Domo embraced her. "I give you this new world for you and for your people. It will be yours forever, and you do not need to worry about invaders again. The Krepts were the last of the war-like peoples. You can live in peace forever, just like you have."

"But what are we to do?" Mioma asked. "The village is certainly lost, and we need others to survive."

Domo smiled. "They have been hiding, but we will go seek them out. Here, give me your hand and we will go."

Mioma looked at the new and strange vegetation before her, the beginning of a new life for her and others. She would miss her friends from the village, but Domo had brought her this far. She knew she could trust the girl to take them further. She hoped that she would never again see the form that Domo had taken standing above the advancing horde, but if it was necessary for the girl to assume that form again, it would be well so long as her Domo returned to her. Domo had made a promise, and somehow Mioma knew that all would be well.

HUNT
By C M Martin

He was looking for sex. He wasn't interested in companionship or tender understanding. He wasn't hoping to build a life with anyone; the very idea was foreign to him. He only wanted—no, needed—to quench the fire that raged through him, a fire that he scarcely understood but which drove him out every night, searching, hoping, burning up with frustrated lust.

It was not easy. There were so many competitors, and they were strong and handsome, sauntering along as if they owned the very earth beneath their feet, and they moved quickly to seize their opportunities. He was slightly smaller than most, not particularly good-looking, and with no other advantages that would tip the scales in his favor. Still, he went out every night, and every night he was hungrier, more desperate. What if he never found her?

On this night, he wandered through the park, looking, always looking for what he needed. There! There up ahead, under that tree. She was alone, and she was hungry, too. He could read it in her body language, in the way she quivered when she spotted him.

He moved nearer, slowly, his eyes locked on her. If he moved too fast, she might be frightened and leave. He couldn't bear it. He couldn't lose her now, not when he was so close to finally quieting the hormonal storm that was almost tearing him apart.

Finally he was close enough to reach out and stroke her face, ever so gently, ever so tenderly. She was stunning: slim and dark, with huge melting eyes and graceful limbs like a dancer. She leaned toward him, silent but obviously receptive. Then she beckoned to him with her eyes and stepped back further under the tree, where the shadows were as deep and rich as velvet, and the grass was plush and soft, a perfect cushion for their bodies. He stumbled after her, hardly able to realize that at long last he was going to gain his desire.

He was clumsy; he had never experienced coitus before. No one had been willing to lie with him, but she was. She had to show him what to do, using soft touches and subtle shifts of position to communicate her desires. His excitement threatened to overwhelm him, but at last he managed to mount her. He thrust hard into her depths, almost overcome with pleasure. She was humming now, a soft counterpart to his thrusts. He was lost in her, drowning in her, unable to do anything but thrust, thrust, thrust as he rocked back and forth upon her body, feeling her inner depths close around him like a sopping velvet glove, squeezing and teasing until he thought he would go insane. She raised her head, and his eyes met hers even as his climax approached. She nestled closer, stretched out her neck---and bit his head off.

As the male shuddered, his body racked with orgasm and death throes, the female Kalmalkean waited until he was still, then she wriggled free of his dead weight and began to feast upon his carcass, pleased by tonight's encounter. She felt the soft cool breeze brush across her scales and drew the scent of wet grass and lilacs deep within her olfactory holes. They had been right to conquer this planet; after the elimination of those inconvenient and dangerous mammals, it had become a paradise. She chewed thoughtfully on a foreleg as she looked down at her mate, her prey, with blank black eyes that showed no emotion other than satisfaction. He had served his purpose. She would bear now, bear hundreds to help repopulate this world they had conquered, and someday her daughters would hunt here as well.

CARRIERS
By Sam Taylor

Private Terry York sat in the midday sun, hot and bothered. She drank eagerly from her water bottle, then hooked it back on her belt. She snapped a long twig off a bush near her perch on a small, rounded boulder and scratched meaningless patterns on a patch of bare ground beneath the rock. She was not watching what she was doing, so was startled to hear a hollow metallic noise from beneath her as the stick scraped across something only millimetres beneath the surface. She squatted down, scraped at the soil with her hands and uncovered a rusty looking metal plate. She inspected it closely for a minute then called out, "Sir?"

"What?!" snapped her Captain, Dale Bryce. He marched over and stared down at her impassively. "Didn't step on a bug, did you?" 'Bugs' were tiny, poison-imbued robots that lay hidden in the soil, often for years, until an unsuspecting boot disturbed them. When their sophisticated sensors detected human movement above, they would erupt from the dirt and seize whatever had disrupted their dormancy, with six small but unyielding arms. The bugs then used a dual-delivery injection system to impale through boots, steel, bone, flesh; whatever they were attached to, and deliver a fast-acting nerve poison. Death usually followed within seconds. Over time, older Bugs would corrode and their poison might leach out before they were ever disturbed, but even a non-deadly sting was agonizing and debilitating.

"No, sir," she said, keeping the irritation from her voice. Bryce hadn't actually sounded all that concerned about whether or not she had stepped on one.

"What then?" he asked tersely.

"There's some sort of inscribed metal plate here under the ground," she informed him.

"So?" he shrugged.

"Shouldn't we investigate it or something; you know, dig it up?"

Bryce laughed, causing York to flush with embarrassment as he sarcastically replied, "Well, you can do whatever you want, Private. Dig away to your heart's content while the rest of us are safe in camp tonight."

The ground beneath her feet buzzed and she froze.

Bryce reacted like a snake, grabbing her and hauling her back as the ground erupted with something much bigger than a Bug.

"What the-" the Captain's voice faltered as they watched the thing rise up. He drew his disruptor.

It was rusty and old, with a cylindrical torso, legs that looked like giant coiled springs, three rickety arms, and a patch of frayed metal and wire where a fourth arm obviously used to reside. It reached for them with large, blunt pincers as it buzzed and flashed weakly, throwing off clods of dirt and grass as it spun back and forth.

"M-mus......p-pro......" it began in a raspy, mechanical voice, but it reverted to a series of dull flashes and hiccupping beeps. It twitched and sputtered on the ground until finally its arms stalled in mid-air and it ceased to move altogether.

York could feel herself shaking. "Shit!" she gasped.

They stared at the robot as Bryce pulled them back a little and blasted the robot. The blaster effect crawled over the surface of the robot then consumed it in a flare of light.

'What did you do that for?" she asked. "We could have just disabled it and accessed its memory banks!"

"I don't like robots," he growled. He realised he was still holding her arm and released her with a glare. "Come on," he ordered, glaring at the rest of his troops for good measure, and they marched forward.

They pushed their way through the thick underbrush beneath a green canopy of trees. The Russian summer grew warmer every year. Although pleasant, it meant that they had their work cut out for them. The terrain in this area was too steep and rugged for their tanks and earthmoving equipment,

170

so foot soldiers were being sent into the new territories in advance of the main army. Bryce's group was one of many such scouting parties. They would be there for months, mapping and searching for areas where the much needed heavy equipment could be dropped in and put to work.

The more territory they lost to the oceanic encroachment in the south, the greater the need to push north into new territories, thus their current scouting assignment. But Captain Bryce was less than enthused. Too often, long term scouting assignments were made even longer by the greed of the Generals and the hunt for valuable resources left behind by civilizations long past. It was random things like the robot that York had unearthed that Bryce hated the most. He hated not knowing what they were going to find next, or whether his next heartbeat would be his last. He would rather be back in his warm tent enjoying a well-earned rest and a beer than hiking through miles of potentially deadly, virgin wilderness.

They were better off than most scouting parties, though, with the luxury of not one but two Sniffers, York and Chensky, in their group. York and Chensky's noses could detect the scent of wolfbears from about a mile away, a peculiar talent which only about two per cent of the population shared.

He turned back to instruct his men, "York and Chenski, if you get a whiff, just a whiff, of wolfbears, you let me know..." he trailed off suddenly, the shocked expressions of his soldiers' faces as they stared wide-eyed over his shoulders, giving him pause. Bryce spun around to see another robot similar to the one they had just unearthed and destroyed. This one, although rusty and dinted, had all six limbs and there was nothing wrong with its voice box. "Must protect! Must protect!" its mechanical voice howled as it surged towards him, snapping green branches and vines out of its way.

Bryce yelled in protest as a pair of pincers grabbed him around the waist and hefted him up high into the air. The robot marched determinedly forward, carrying him through his men, who scattered and looked on in confusion and panic. The chanting robot and the raging human moved rapidly back down the path from where the scouting party had just come.

"Don't shoot!" Sargeant Jim Davis yelled, reaching up to push York's arm down at the last minute. The disruptor charge she fired crackled harmlessly over a dead tree trunk before disintegrating it.

"Why not?" she snapped, jogging off after the robot and its unwilling cargo.

"The new disruptors, remember? You would have killed the Captain!" the older man reminded her.

He was right, she realised. The new disruptors had sensors which, when they hit, expanded their disruption net over anything that was connected to their target and moving.

Davis pulled out his old disruptor and fired off several shots, all of which missed, striking the trees and rocks instead of their target.

York grumbled at him, "You'd be a useful sniper if you could still see, old man."

He snarled something she didn't hear at her as they jogged along. It sounded rude. She grinned.

Five kilometres of jogging, and York's chest was beginning to burn and her legs to ache despite her fitness. Davis, although older, was still running easily along just ahead of her in a ground-eating lope that belied his years. She glared at him, and muttered grudgingly, "Tough old fart."

The rest of their group was strung out about twenty to fifty metres behind them, puffing and panting but determined not to get left behind. York glanced back anxiously and sniffed the air around them quite a few times. The wolfbears were always on the watch for stragglers. Bryce's team had discovered that the hard way the week before, when a small wolfbear pack had reduced their numbers by three. The wolfbears had come in from downwind, so York and Chensky's sensitive noses had not detected the distinctive odour of the predators until it was too late. The team had doubled back, but by the time they got to the stragglers there was nothing left of the three young soldiers, only bloodied grass in the clearing. York could not forget the awful feeling of culpability; she and Chensky with their sensitive noses were supposed to be the group's insurance against just such an event. Captain Bryce had shot her an enquiring look as they all walked away. He had not reprimanded her or Chensky, but she had wished many times since that he had; his silence was worse.

She was brought roughly out of her reverie when she collided unexpectedly with Davis's back and it momentarily knocked the wind from her lungs. He put an arm back to steady her. They stared, incredulous, as the robot set its burden down with remarkable gentleness. Captain Bryce groaned audibly and rolled over. *At least he's still alive*, she thought.

Davis pushed York off the immediate path. "Clear the way!" he shouted to the others as they came rushing up the slope. The robot had turned around a hundred and eighty degrees and was trotting back in their direction. York's heart hammered in her chest as the robot slowed and marched toward them. When it finally stopped, it bent to peer at her face from just centimetres away. She slowly began to reach for the disruptor on her belt, but Davis's hand clamped onto hers to stall the action. The robot's eyes were huge, liquid pools of silver. Its gaze moved over them all as it repeated in a quiet, low tone, "Must protect. Must protect."

It seemed to make some sort of decision before abruptly leaving them and continuing along the path. There were a few shouts as it scattered the rest of their contingent out of its way, then buzzed its busy way out of sight.

Bryce had recovered enough to be swearing up a storm of invectives as he dusted himself off and brushed away York's proffered hand. When Davis offered to help him to his feet, however, York noticed that Bryce did not push him away. He gave the Sargeant a brief, grateful look before rounding on the rest of his team to glare at them all. "Well, fat lot of use you lot are!" he barked. "What were you going to do, wait 'til the bloody thing dragged me into a cave and made love to me before you got your heads out of your asses and did something?"

York couldn't suppress the giggle that escaped her, and Bryce turned his ire on her. She cringed inwardly as he asked icily, "Do you have something useful to say, Private York?"

Davis snorted, then the whole team cracked up laughing. Bryce stomped off yelling, "You're all on report. And demoted!"

York looked at Davis, who shrugged. "Don't worry, he'll get over it when he gets to blast a few robots. He really hates robots."

York sighed, then grumbled, "Yeah, but now he's in a foul mood and we're all exhausted from running after him. It's going to be a rough afternoon."

The older man patted her on the shoulder and said, "Come on, we'll go find you both something to shoot to take your mind off your worries."

She sighed, a little relieved but mostly just exhausted, and followed him back up the path.

They followed Bryce, pushing through the exhausted group of soldiers to start back on the trail they had cut earlier. They made their way along the path until they were nearly back to the area where they had found the first robot. More and more of the robots were now emerging from the dense undergrowth and approaching their group. Bryce grumbled, "Looks like that one earlier had time to call in reinforcements."

Bryce pulled out his disruptor and disintegrated three robots before they got close enough to grab any of his men, but the machines were quick learners. As the soldiers rushed along the path, the robots began to ambush them from the dense shrubbery on either side. Private Chensky cried out from just behind Bryce as he was hoisted off his feet and carried back along the path. Chensky pulled out his disruptor and aimed it at the robot carrying him, but Bryce dialled his weapon down and stunned the lad before he could shoot.

"You can't shoot them once they've picked you up!" Bryce yelled to the rest of his men. "Your own disruptor fire will engulf both of you! If you get picked up just ride it out!" He muttered to Davis, "Now you see why I didn't like Fox's latest upgrades on these disruptors?"

Davis nodded, "Good luck getting that desk jockey to take any notice of what you or I say." He turned to walk ahead of Bryce up the path.

Bryce dialed his disruptor back up to maximum and followed, only to be confronted by another robot which crashed through the undergrowth onto the path between him and Davis. If he shot it, he risked the disrupter's halo engulfing Davis who was standing right behind it. Bryce stepped back, trying to put some space between himself and the robot and draw it away from his Sargeant. He stumbled awkwardly out of reach of its grasping arms, but his foot caught on something and he tripped. He heard a distinctive double beep and knew exactly what he had stumbled over.

Bryce rolled to the side as a small, deadly Bug erupted from the ground, spun and scurried toward his feet. He scooted backwards hastily but came up against a fallen tree. He could not scramble back any further, only stare in horror as the deadly little Bug closed in.

Suddenly, there was a flash of blue light and the Bug disintegrated just before it reached his foot. He stared up, shocked, at one of the large robots as it holstered a disruptor and reached its mechanical arms down to pick him up. Bryce had the presence of mind to yell to his men at the top of his lungs, "They've got weapons!" Then he groaned as the robot hoisted him over its head and he realized he was in for his second ride of the day. "Must protect," chanted the robot busily as it moved along, bumping and bruising Bryce with its clumsy, steel grip.

Davis heard Bryce's shouted warning and looked around at the robots which were being blasted into oblivion by the scouting party. He frowned, puzzled, as he muttered to himself, "If they have weapons, then why aren't they using them to defend themselves?"

The robot carrying Bryce manhandled the Captain past

Davis and York, and the Sargeant couldn't help himself. "Too lazy to walk, Captain?" he called.

The string of language their commanding officer emitted made his earlier diatribe seem mild. Davis wondered if it was directed at him or the robot, which had begun to chant, "Must protect. Must protect."

Bryce had already endured five kilometres of listening to the incessant chant. So, as he was carted off yet again, he pleaded desperately, "Will you shut the hell UP?" Two other soldiers had also been picked up by the robots and were being carried back along the path in the same direction as Bryce.

Davis called out, "Alpha group, fall in!"

The tired soldiers seemed relieved, and one of the more veteran men said to the robot he had been about to shoot, "Here, give us a lift, Bozo!" The robot complied and some of the other soldiers did the same, allowing themselves to be carted off by the tireless machines. They were all deposited about thirty minutes later precisely where the first robot had left Bryce an hour before.

When they reached him, Bryce was sitting on a rock, watching his carrier robot depart. A frown creased his forehead as he watched Davis and York arrive together, having been collected by two robots. He waited until they were deposited on the ground and the robots began their return to what must be their assigned posts.

"What on earth are they protecting?" wondered Bryce aloud.

Davis shook his head, "I have no idea."

They tried again, fanning out away from the path, approaching from different directions. The robots were everywhere. The results were the same. They were all getting sick of being carried around and the light was fading fast.

"We're getting nowhere," grizzled Bryce, rubbing at the bruises on his arms.

York shook her head, "Um, sir…."

"Shut up, Private," Bryce snapped at her, and she

subsided into silence.

Davis shot her a sympathetic look, and suggested, "Well, this seems like the logical place to set up camp then?"

Bryce glared at him and nodded, but sat staring at the robots standing in the distance. He looked thoughtful and thoroughly peeved. His men noticed and gave him a wide berth as they busied themselves around him, setting up camp for the night.

Davis was sitting relaxing on a boulder, clutching his coffee, when Bryce came and sat next to him. The older man waited.

Bryce finally said, "We just got our orders."

Davis sighed, "We're to go in?"

"Yes."

"Dale... do you really think that's wise?"

"I spoke to General Fox. He said whatever it is they're protecting, it must be valuable. These are pre-reform robots, almost seven hundred years old, from what Headquarters is saying. For them to set up to protect something like that, for such a long period of time, to throw so many resources at it... whatever it is must be worth a mint."

"Might be a mint," Davis pointed out.

Bryce replied, "Could be. Anyway, I've triangulated all the vectors that the robots took to cart our people away from this, whatever 'this' is. Have a look at the schematic." The younger man pushed his pocket Padd towards Davis. Davis took it in his hand and peered at the image.

Bryce went on, pointing at a place on the screen, "All the paths they took when they were carrying our men radiated out from here. So this point in the middle here, must be the location of whatever it is they're trying to protect."

A quiet female voice sounded behind them and both men jumped edgily, "You're assuming they're trying to protect 'something' sirs."

"Jesus, York, don't sneak up on us like that! You'll be lucky if you don't get shot," admonished Bryce. Davis smiled to himself but said nothing and looked down.

"Sorry, Sir. But, permission to speak?"

"Go ahead." Bryce glanced around, then added quietly, "Here, sit down," and indicated a rock opposite where he and Davis were seated.

She sat down and pursed her lips, her dark hair falling over her eyes as she spoke, "Captain, if these robots were assigned to protect whatever is at the core of their territory, then why would they let their numbers be diminished? Robot programming is very straightforward."

"Go on," said Bryce. Davis smiled knowingly to himself, noticing the gentler tone the Captain used with York when he thought no one else would hear.

"Today we destroyed about fifty of them," she continued with more confidence, emboldened by his request for more of her input. "If we keep going, we'll destroy them all. They're not defending themselves."

Bryce and Davis nodded, listening.

"They have weapons, so you'd think if they were protecting something in the centre of that territory, they'd be programmed to protect themselves," she explained, "so that whatever it is, isn't left unguarded eventually."

"But they haven't used their weapons," agreed Bryce slowly, "not against us."

"Why not?" Davis wondered aloud.

Bryce looked at them both pointedly. "They did use them, that's how we know they have them. But only once, and against a Bug."

"Why would a Bug attack a robot?" asked York, looking perplexed.

"It didn't, it attacked me," the Captain explained, "and it would have killed me, but the robot that was trying to pick me up shot it."

"What, so the robot was protecting you against the Bug?" asked York, her eyes wide.

They all fell silent, brows creased. Then, Davis looked at the others, his face alight. "Must protect!" he exclaimed. "Damn, I'm an idiot."

"What?" the two younger officers asked in unison.

Davis replied, watching their faces carefully, "What if 'must protect' means they must protect... us?"

Bryce and York looked thoughtful, then the Captain asked, "But how do they even know we exist? I mean, that we would exist. These robots were left here nearly seven hundred years ago."

"It fits with what it did to the Bug," mused York.

"But why would they keep taking us away from whatever it is they're guarding out there?" Bryce questioned, "Why keep us from it? Shouldn't they want us to have it?"

York looked excited, "What if it's treasure? What if it really is the ancient Russian mint?"

Davis was shaking his head, and countered, "What if it's dangerous?"

They all fell silent, looking thoughtful.

"Damn," whispered Bryce.

York looked abashed, but began to nod slowly as she thought it through, "I think you might have hit the nail on the head, Sargeant. Robots are logical if nothing else, and that fits all the information we have so far."

Davis was nodding now as well, "Whatever it is, I bet it's a death-trap."

Bryce looked worried, "I have my orders though. We have to go in there."

"Contact Headquarters and explain. Surely Fox will understand our position," suggested Davis.

Bryce shot him a quizzical look, and Davis added, "Yeah, well, we can only try."

"I'll try," said Bryce as he began to walk off with his pocket Padd. However, before he had taken more than a few steps, he turned and looked back at York and Davis. He walked back to them slowly, looking Davis in the eye. "But your orders, regardless of what answer I get back from Headquarters," he instructed quietly, "are to take her, and get out. Take my survival igloo, you'll need it if she senses wolfbears."

The survival igloo was a device about the size of a person's hand which when deployed became a small but impenetrable forcefield igloo with enough space for two people. Bryce had found it many years ago when surveying a Himalayan temple with Davis.

"Sir?" York was stunned.

"Shh," Davis hushed her. He nodded at Bryce, and asked, "What do I tell them back at base camp?"

"You outline our concerns and say I ordered you to go back, so that someone with full knowledge of the situation could take the news to Headquarters. I'll give you a chip with written orders."

"Sir, we are not turning back without you!" York's face was red as she stood up to the Captain.

Their faces were millimetres apart as Bryce stared down his nose at her. His gave his order in a huff of breath that brushed across her cheeks, "Yes… you are."

She glared at him evenly, but remembered that he was her superior officer, and finally asked in a small voice, "Why Sargeant Davis and me?"

Rather than answer, he stepped forward and closed the distance between them. With one warm hand secured at the back of her neck and his other still clutching his Padd he pulled her to him quickly and surprised her with a hard, fast kiss. Then, just as quickly, he pulled away and marched off without another word. She stood staring after him, gaping.

Davis laughed as he said, "Bet you didn't see that coming, did you?"

She managed to shake her head while Davis yelled after their retreating Captain, "Hey, where's my kiss, you insensitive jerk?"

He chuckled loudly when the Captain's retort reached his ears, a resounding: "Get lost!"

The older man grinned and turned to the still stunned woman beside him. "See, he does love me."

She turned to him and he grinned wider. "You gonna stand there all night catching flies with your mouth? Come on," he said, his tone switching from teasing to serious instantly, "we'd better pack up and get going."

She wordlessly followed him back to the tents.

In the morning, Captain Bryce was all business. Other groups had arrived in the night, not long after he had filed his report of the prior day's events. Headquarters had responded predictably to the one motivation which always seemed to jolt it out of its general ennui: greed. They were to advance against the robots immediately.

Bryce turned to stare for a moment at the faces of the younger men in his contingent. Chensky was talking into his pocket Padd and grinning like a Cheshire cat. Bryce knew he had an older brother back at the base camp. Chensky was excited because their furloughs would coincide next week, and Bryce smiled quietly to himself. He glanced up one final time at the hills where he knew Davis and York would be hours away by now. He returned his focus to the men before him and called them to attention. "Our orders are simple: Defeat the robots guarding the inner perimeter shown on your handhelds. The General and his men will then advance into the centre of their territory. Move out!"

With the reinforcements at their back and the knowledge they had gathered about the robots the day before, the battle went much more smoothly. They discovered that if a robot saw a human collapse it would march out to help, putting itself well within blaster range.

Finally, General Fox arrived just as the last robots were being destroyed. He considered the complex of low buildings in the distance before directing his companies to advance into the inner perimeter and explore the grounds.

General Fox led his group into the largest of the buildings once it was cleared by the advance teams. He arrived at what appeared to be a computer complex and waved a group of his men towards the array of now-yellowed plastic cases. Mice and rats had chewed the exposed wiring, and he knew it would be many hours before his technicians had the systems up and running. In the meantime, he went with the group that was exploring the rest of the compound. "Find me anything of value. Gold, art works, information… there must have been something here that they wanted to protect," he grumbled at his minions. He knew that opportunities like this came along only once in a decade, and he rubbed his hands in anticipation.

When, after nearly an hour of tediously searching each building, another room yielded only petri dishes and test tubes, Fox's patience was beginning to wane. He smashed the equipment angrily as he roared with annoyance, "Nothing!"

"Son of a…!" Fox shouted suddenly with a jolt, gripping his forearm in pain. One of the test tubes had cut his arm. He wiped the blood from his arm angrily, then demanded, "Where's Captain Bryce? He might know something more, he's been in on this assignment from the get-go."

A young orderly answered nervously, "I haven't seen him, sir."

"Well, go find him!" roared the General, throwing a test tube at the boy, who ran off, relieved to be out of his presence.

Fox turned and surveyed the room, then smiled as he spotted a large, heavy door in a side wall. He made his way to it and called three technicians over, "Is that a safe?"

When they nodded, he snapped impatiently at them, "Well, don't just stare at it! Crack it!"

The technicians pulled listening devices out of their kits and began the process of cracking the safe. After a minute, Fox lost interest and looked around. "Where's that orderly?"

No sooner had he voiced his question did the young man appear in the main entry, looking flustered.

"Well? Did you find Captain Bryce?" demanded Fox.

"I'm sorry, sir, no-one has seen him. We think his group may have been amongst those who were fighting back the last of the robots in the gorge that runs down off the plateau. It may be some hours before they climb back up."

"Hours? It'll be days. That gorge is steep as hell. It leads down off this plateau into the foothills. If Bryce has any brains, he'll keep going down and rendezvous with us back at the base camp in a few days." Fox growled at the orderly, "Dismissed."

Down near the end of the deep gorge, Captain Bryce faced the last of the robots. It had fallen into a crack in the rock, and its mechanical legs were thoroughly jammed, immobilising it. Its hands were free, yet it made no attempt to raise its weapon at Bryce. Its liquid silver eyes gazed impassively at him, and he hesitated before raising his disruptor as an idea formed in his mind. He walked up to the robot and asked it, "What are you protecting?"

The robot intoned, "Nothing."

Bryce shook his head, frustrated, and raised his disruptor. But then he felt a hand on his arm and turned to see Chensky looking at him eagerly. The kid did everything eagerly. He reminded Bryce of an excitable puppy.

"What?" Bryce asked.

"If you will allow me, sir, I think I can get some information out of it. I majored in Robotic History at the Academy."

Bryce shrugged and stepped back. Chensky turned to the trapped robot and asked, "What are you protecting?"

"Nothing," came the mechanical reply.

Chensky tilted his head, puzzled, then his eyes lit up and he said, "Who are you protecting?"

The robot looked down at its jammed legs and repeated, "Nobody."

Chensky was on top of that response quickly, Bryce noted. The kid was no dunce. Chensky asked, "Who are you programmed to protect?"

"Humans," came the vague reply.

"The humans in those buildings up there?" Bryce couldn't help interrupting, his curiosity getting the better of him.

"There are no humans left there," said the robot.

"Then what humans? Please specify. Give names or descriptions," Chensky pressed.

"You."

Bryce raised his eyes to the skies, "Forget it, kid, the thing's obviously so rudimentarily programmed it doesn't know one human from another."

"Sir, with all due respect, there is often little apparent difference between rudimentary programming and system override programming. I think this may be the latter," suggested Chensky.

"What?" Bryce questioned irritably. "Why would a robot be programmed to protect all humans? I've never heard such rot."

"Listen," Chensky insisted, momentarily forgetting his rank. "Please, Sir," he added.

"Okay."

Chensky turned back to the robot and said clearly, "Anything less than full and immediate disclosure of the specifics of your protective function will result in our certain deaths."

The robot clicked and whirred for several moments and then began, "In the year 2056, there was born a man called Raminoff- "

Raminoff was the inventor of the robotic random cascade brain which mimicked human thought. Chensky groaned, and Bryce chuckled, "You did say full disclosure, kid."

"Sorry, sir," Chensky responded tiredly before stopping the robot, "Desist. Specify in five sentences why you are programmed to protect us and what specific protection we need now."

The robot hummed busily, giving the appearance of happiness in an odd, robotic way, "All biological life is precious. Humans are the most precious creatures of all. Humans have souls, which are beyond robotic comprehension." There was a pause, then its voice changed to what sounded like a recording of a male human voice, "The disease is out. You need to get the hell out and stay out."

Bryce frowned, "What?"

Chensky paled, "What is your hierarchy of action to

protect humans?"

Bryce had fallen silent.

The robot replied almost instantly, "Block, remove, deny access, immobilize, sterilize."

"Well, we already know how they do the first three," commented Bryce wryly, "I wonder how they immobilize and sterilize? It must be their last resort."

"Specify methods for immobilization and sterilization." Chensky was looking very, very pale now.

"Last resort?" the robot repeated, then looked up at them, "Is this unit the last robot?"

Bryce opened his mouth, but Chensky jumped over and slapped his hand over the Captain's mouth, and lied, "NO. No, you are not the last robot."

Bryce's eyes were like saucers as Chensky gave him an apologetic look, before he released him and turned back to the robot, "What is the prescribed method for sterilization?"

"This unit does not have that information. Only the central computer has that information," replied the robot, and Chensky breathed a sigh of relief. He turned to Bryce, "It's okay, I didn't want it to send a message back to its base to start some sort of doomsday countdown, sorry sir."

Bryce stared at him, then said, "I think we'd better contact Fox." He turned to reach for his pocket Padd.

The robot suddenly asked, unbidden, "Are there now humans at the central compound?"

Bryce and Chensky looked at each other in sudden concern, and Bryce turned back to face the robot.

"Why do you ask?" replied Chensky evasively.

Then Chensky jumped as Bryce drew his disruptor and vaporized the robot. He turned to Bryce indignantly. The Captain looked at him and said, "I didn't like the way that conversation was going. Let's contact Headquarters."

He took out his pocket Padd, but found to his frustration that the sides of the steep, winding gorge were so high that there was no signal. He shook it angrily and said, "I have a funny feeling we should warn Fox."

They stared up at the steep escarpment above them, and Chensky commented, "You know, it's going to be a hard slog getting back up there."

Bryce nodded vaguely and stared at the young man for a long time, lost in thought before he roused himself, deciding, "It would be easier on the men to keep going down this gorge and back out to the base camp. Probably just as quick, too."

Bryce called the rest of their forces in and watched them shuffle up, all of them looking exhausted after their long morning fighting in the steep terrain. "Line up. March, double-time," he called, and led them off at a jog. Chensky and the others stared at him incredulously, but obeyed after only a few seconds. Bryce led them along at a merciless pace for hours, and as evening approached Chensky puffed his way up to Bryce, and managed to ask, "Sir? Is there any reason for the hard run? The men are exhausted. I thought you said you wanted to go easy on them?"

Bryce just shook his head, and replied quietly, "Trust me son, I've got a gut feeling about this."

They were about twenty kilometres out from the compound by nightfall, and Chensky was stumbling along in a daze of exhaustion. To his surprise, Bryce took his arm and helped him along to a small ravine with several caves at its base. "We'll camp in the caves." The men collapsed outside the entrances gratefully, but Bryce hounded them deeper into the caves.

Chensky walked over to Bryce in the fading light and flopped down beside him on the cave floor, looking curiously at his Captain. He inquired hesitantly, "Sir?"

Bryce raised weary eyebrows at him, and said, "You want to know what the hell's going on, don't you, son?"

"I wouldn't presume to question your command, sir," answered Chensky carefully.

"No, but I can hear the 'but' on the end of that sentence," Bryce smiled. He fell silent for a while, then spoke quietly, so the others wouldn't hear him, "You see, it's like this. Most emotions fade as you get older. But there are some, that get stronger; just a couple. Not necessarily the good ones."

Chensky frowned, looking puzzled, "Sir?"

"Greed, Chensky."

"Greed, sir?"

"Yes. It's one of the emotions that gets stronger as you get older. In an old man like Fox, it's a fire in his belly. But I'm not that old. I've got people I...." he stopped, and glanced over at the younger man, "Well, let's just say I'm not blinded by greed."

"I-I don't understand, sir."

Bryce looked out at the fading light coming in through the cave entrance, "I hope I'm wrong, Chensky. I hope to hell I'm wrong."

Back at the compound, General Fox stared at the medic in front of him incredulously, "Sick? But Meadows was fine an hour ago."

"Sir, there seems to be some sort of illness spreading very rapidly among the men," the medic informed him anxiously. "It's fast, and it's bad. We were hoping that if you had accessed the main computers, we might find something in there about it."

Fox looked worried, "My technicians should have access in about another ten minutes. Come on." He led the medic and his two assistants quickly through the complex from his temporary office towards the main computer room.

"What are the main symptoms?" Fox asked the medic as they strode along.

"Blue blotches under the arms and severe breathing difficulties, sir," responded the medic. Fox nodded as they arrived at the main computer room.

A technician greeted him and led him to the main screen, advising, "We think we have it going now, sir. We should be able to access the memory banks in less than a minute."

Fox glanced about him as they waited and noticed belatedly the signs of illness in the people around him; a flushed face here, a muted cough there. It wasn't anything that any of the soldiers would complain about yet, but if what the medics were telling him was accurate, it could get very serious, very quickly.

The head tech looked at Fox and gestured an invitation to him, as the main computer screen irised into activity. Fox peered into the screen, and the computer identified a human retina. Its mechanical voice inquired, "You are human?"

"Yes," answered Fox, a little puzzled. What else would he be?

"Computing GPS coordinates…. identical. This computer is still located in the main complex at GenFlex?"

The tech leaned over closer to the General and said, "Yes, sir, that is what this complex is called."

"Are any of the humans ill?" asked the computer voice, "Do any exhibit blue blotches under the arms and severe respiratory symptoms?"

Fox looked surprised, but pleased. Evidently they would find the information they needed to cure the illness. Maybe they would find other, more valuable medical information too, "Yes!" he confirmed, "We have many soldiers ill already. Do you have information on how to deal with this illness?"

"Yes, that is part of my programming," intoned the computer, and the medic beside Fox tilted his head, wondering if he were imagining a note of sadness in the computer mainframe voice.

Beneath their very feet ran a series of communication fibres which the technicians had not yet discovered, encased as they were in solid concrete and stone for their entire length. The fibres led straight down through the concrete column supporting the mainframe and into the solid rock below. A pulse of code, unbeknownst to the men above, lit up those fibres nexus by nexus. Down and down through the solid rock they led, to an explosives bunker below.

"Sterilize," said the computer.

"What—" Fox began, but was never able to finish.

Back at the base camp, Davis and York threw themselves

down and covered their eyes. Luckily for them, they were just outside the blast radius and immediate fallout area. Even more luckily, the wind blew in the other direction for the next few evenings.

The next morning, York was incredulous when she found Davis suiting up to enter the blast zone, "Are you mad? You won't last five hours in there!"

"So I'm mad."

She stared at him as he zipped up his suit, "What possible hope could they have had in that? As far as we know Dale was heading right into Ground Zero."

"I should never have left him there," muttered the older man quietly.

"You won't come back," she pointed out.

"Suits me."

A quiet voice behind them said, "Do I get a say in this?"

York sobbed in relief and threw herself at Bryce, who winced as she hugged him. "Easy there, young-un," he groaned.

Davis was standing transfixed, staring at Bryce. The Captain's face looked sunburnt, and he was still wet from a decontamination shower. Slowly Davis walked up to him and asked, "How...?"

Bryce said simply, "Sheer luck and gut instinct. You were going in there to get me?" He ignored York to stare at Davis.

"Yes."

Bryce pulled Davis against himself with one arm and said, "Idiot." Then, impulsively, he planted an affectionate kiss on the older man's forehead.

Davis grinned wickedly at York, "See? I got my kiss after all!"

Bryce asked, "Did Fox...?"

Davis shook his head, "Fox got what he deserved. The only thing is, he took a lot of good people with him."

"And a lot of good robots," said Bryce sadly, and the others both looked at him in surprise.

Edited by Sam Taylor

ABOUT THE AUTHORS

Patricia Burn (Cover art and poem Space Cadet)
Patricia has an Honours Degree in both Politics and Literature and has been many things to many people. A polymath with an altruistic streak she is at her happiest listening to music whilst creating art.
Website: www.patriciaburn.com

Salvatore B Lombard (Shipping and Handling)
A Classics student who enjoys studying language, Salvatore spends his free time doodling cartoons and picking up horse poop.

Daniel Z. Klein (Fruit of Memory)
Daniel is a German video game designer who inexplicably can't stop writing fiction in English. Normally it's dirtier, and more people die, but he behaved this time.

Rachael Kelly (Blumelena)
An award-winning author from Northern Ireland, Rachael has a PhD in film theory and a mild obsession with Marcus Antonius, and her first non-fiction book (which features both of these things) will be published in 2013.

John Gribbin (Artifact)
John Gribbin writes science fiction based on fact, and science fact that reads like fiction. He also writes songs for the group 'Three Bonzos and a Piano.'
Website: www.johngribbinbooks.com

C. M. Martin (Orientation, Hunt)
When not writing, teaching, crafting or plotting world domination, Martin fulfils her destiny as the indentured servant of four cats and two ferrets.
Website: cymartin.wix.com/cmmcr

Kelli Faust (Eighth Day)
Kelli Faust grew up in a family of astronomers and has always been intrigued by science fact and the visions of science fiction. She has a degree in Biotechnology and lives a relatively normal life in suburbia with her husband and three opinionated cats.

Kate Welty (Eartholder)
Kate's real life, her passionate internal life, has always leapt and wept, laughed and stormed within the fictions of other writers' stories; there she lived joyfully within their realities. Now, inexplicably, she is creating stories. Perhaps that is good. It is certainly interesting.

Debbie Painter (Domo)
A graduate of the University of Tennessee Knoxville, Debbie was employed for many years by the State of Tennessee. Upon retirement, she is trying a new field – writing.
Website: www.debbiepainter.com

Sam Taylor (Editor, and story Carriers)
Sam Taylor is an Australian science fiction author who has written over 98 short stories and the novels 'Deadly Jewel' and 'the Eye of Shiva.' Sam has a Master's degree in science. For more information see the Perseus website: www.talesfromtheperseusarm.com

WHAT IS THE PERSEUS PROJECT?

The Perseus Project aims to bring readers new and exciting stories from the best writers in science fiction.

For more information on upcoming volumes and our authors, or to read Sam's reluctant blog, find us here:

Website: www.talesfromtheperseusarm.com

(includes blog)

Twitter: @theperseusarm

Facebook: www.facebook.com/talesfromperseus

Authors: to enquire about submitting a story for future editions: email Sam Taylor at deadlyjewel@hotmail.com.

Edited by Sam Taylor

Complete your collection – Vol 2 **available now**, Vol 3 *coming soon*

Edited by Sam Taylor

SGA Publications
www.sgapublications.com

Services for authors:
Manuscript Assessment
Editing and Proof Reading
eBook and Print Publishing
Marketing and Distribution

**All our books are available in print and kindle
format at www.amazon.com**

www.ingramcontent.com/pod-product-compliance
Lightning Source LLC
Chambersburg PA
CBHW070017260626
47159CB00005B/1839